DISC

ICEBLINK

ICEBLINK

RUTHERFORD MONTGOMERY

ILLUSTRATED BY

RUDOLF FREUND

Questions and related activities by **Jennifer Harvey, B.A.**

a publication of

THE BOOK SOCIETY OF CANADA
Limited

Agincourt   Canada

Printed in Canada

1 2 3 4 5 6 7 76 75 74 73 72 71 70 69

CONTENTS

5

ASIA

THE PETR FROZEN IN ★

POINT BARROW

★ METE
HOME

EIBER VILLAGE ★

CAPE
LISBURNE

STRAIT

DIOMEDES

BERING

NORTON SOUND

ALASKA

Y-U-K-O-N

NUSHUGAK

METEK'S VOYAGE

VOYAGE OF THE PETR

BERING

SEA

BRISTOL
BAY

ALEUTIAN ISLANDS

★ METEK JOINS
THE
PETR

A MAP OF
METEK'S
JOURNEY

1. FAMINE

To the west lay Point Barrow, its rocky tip pointing to the north pole. Above the barren shore line rose low cliffs, standing like shadows in the gloom of the arctic night. Ten days had passed since the sun, a dull red ball of almost no warmth, had dipped into the tumbled mass of ice which was the sea. Now there was only the arctic stars, Cassiopeia, Orion and the carpet of the Milky Way to light the land of snow and ice.

7

Metek sat on a snowdrift, his arms around the neck of his husky dog, Karsuk. Metek was hungry with a gnawing lankness that twisted and pulled inside him. In all of his fifteen years of life he had never before met so stark a threat of starvation. Many times he had been hungry, very hungry, but never like this, weak and cramped inside.

Etah, his father, was the greatest hunter among all the Innuits living near the point, and his household was seldom without meat. Rarely was he unable to bring in walrus or seal or fox or bear for the glowing *kotluck* over which his mother cooked their food. But this was a winter such as few, even among the old men, could recall. There was no open water so there was no walrus. The little foxes seemed to have vanished; the white bear shunned the jutting headlands. And Took-too, the long-horned caribou, had marched far up into the high hills seeking ridges where the wind had swept the snow from the lichens and mosses.

Karsuk growled deep in his shaggy chest and tried to lick Metek's face. He seemed to understand that trouble had overtaken his master. He was more starved than Metek because he had been without food much longer. He had eaten only once in a week. That meal had been a bearskin boot he had stolen from the hut. He was uneasy and restless because he was the last dog left in the village. The others had died, one after another, under the knives of the hungry natives. Their stringy carcasses had held at bay the grim, white specter known so well in this land of cold and dusk, the fearful one, hunger.

And now Karsuk alone remained, and Metek knew that soon, within another day, his father would be forced to kill the big one so that the family might eat. His mother had tossed the last scrap of meat, a piece from the skeleton of a fox, into the *kolopsuts* for their evening meal. Metek pulled the big dog closer to him. He was sure that, in spite of his hunger, he would choke if he tried to swallow a bite of meat from the dog.

Karsuk whined a little and rubbed his head against Metek's hood. He was a big, savage animal with a shaggy, red coat trimmed with snuff-colored facings. His ears were short and erect and his muzzle wide and black. When he ran, his tail always curled up over his back like a coiled spring. Metek had raised him from puppyhood. He was Metek's own dog and he pulled the boy's sled. Once Karsuk had been king-dog of a swift team. In the space of a few minutes he could trounce any dog in the village. But he was a cunning leader and could scent a conspiracy against his stern rule before it was well started. Revolts against his kingship had always been put down with savage promptness. Every dog in the village had hated him, but few had ever challenged him. Now that the others were dead Karsuk was restless.

"If we could go out across the ice and find open water or hear a seal blowing under the ice you would be saved," Metek said slowly.

He had thought about going out alone with his dog. It would be a foolish thing to do. The greatest hunters in the village had traveled north and south, east and west. His father had gone many miles farther than any of the others. They had seen nothing but high, piled bergs, snow-choked valleys between up-ended ice rafts where the great floes had crashed together in their voyage out of the frozen sea. Metek had never made a long run alone. He had gone many times with his father and was considered a man, but he had never been sent alone. He knew the dangers and how you met them. The worst of all the forces of the Arctic is the wind which drives the cold through fur clothing.

Metek knew what to do when the wind caught you on a lonely ice field. He knew all of the things a hunter

learns. When the wind came, lashing the still air into fury,
your fur parka, bearskin pantaloons and hood would not
save you. You must burrow into a snow bank and lie there
until the wind wore itself out. Sometimes the wind did
not wear itself out for days and you could not come out,
no matter how hungry or thirsty you got. Thirsty, yes,
you got very thirsty because the snow took up the salt
from the ice. Metek scowled out across the dim ocean,
the sea that was refusing his people food.

Something was happening to the ice floes. Suddenly
a bright light darted up from behind a black cloud that
lay low on the horizon. It lasted but an instant and, having
filled the air with brightness, vanished. Almost at once
an arch of light flooded upward, springing across the sky
in wavering bands of light. The space enclosed by the arch
was very dark and filled by the black cloud.

By degrees the light grew more and more intense,
settling into a steady sheet of brightness. The broad dome
above Metek and Karsuk was all ablaze. Blue and yellow
streamers played in the lurid fire which cast a ghostly,
green glare over the landscape and the sea. The weird
forms of countless bergs loomed above the ice pack. The
scene was noiseless, yet Metek imagined he heard a sound
like the beating of great wings.

Karsuk lifted his muzzle to the polar star and howled
long and mournfully, the howl of his ancestors, the wolves,
a defiant and sad burst of song. Metek rubbed the dog's
head and blunt muzzle. Perhaps this was a sign. It was the
first great aurora in many days.

Then the wind came rushing in from the sea. It stabbed
the cold through Metek's parka, chilling him at once. He
got to his feet and turned toward the doorway of his
father's hut. He must retreat into the warmth of his home.

Karsuk would burrow down into a snowdrift and curl up. He patted the dog's head.

"I will think hard, perhaps there will be a way," he said softly. But a feeling within him said that Karsuk was doomed.

Facing what appeared to be a high bank of snow, he dropped to his hands and knees. Before him were two dirt-marked holes in the snow. These were the door and the window of his home. Metek ducked into the lower hole. He crawled along a passageway some thirty paces in length and came to the room where he lived.

The hut measured fifteen feet in length by six feet in width. It was filled with steam from human bodies. The room was hot, the temperature standing at close to ninety degrees. Metek slipped out of his heavy clothing at once.

Metek's father and mother, his seven brothers and sisters, and the family of Eiderduck sat or lay on the floor. Eiderduck with his wife and five children had moved in with Etah when the first food shortage struck the village. Eiderduck was a very poor hunter and a very poor home builder, but true to Innuit custom, he and his family were made welcome. They shared the warmth and what food there was equally with the others. They had not been invited to come and they were not asked to stay, but they would not be put out nor would they be refused an equal share of any meat there was to be eaten.

Metek seated himself beside his father. He was the eldest son and that was his place. Etah did not look at his son; he was watching little Noogak, the baby. Little Noogak should have been fat and round like a baby seal, instead she was thin and her legs were skinny. Metek knew his father was thinking Noogak needed meat to stop her crying.

Then Etah spoke to his wife. Still he did not look at Metek.

"We will sleep. In the morning I will prepare the last of the meat. The little ones must eat."

Metek's face showed no trace of his feelings any more than his father's face showed how he felt. His mother nodded, then she looked at Metek and her dark eyes were soft and filled with sorrow. She knew how much Karsuk meant to her boy.

Everyone stretched out on the floor, covering it so that the children curled up close against each other. Metek lay down beside his father. In a short time silence filled the hut, broken only by the uneasy snores and the low mutterings caused by empty stomachs.

Metek did not sleep. He lay with his eyes open staring up into the hot darkness. He did not want to go to sleep because when he wakened Karsuk would be dead. His father would be up before any of the others to have the meat ready for the morning meal.

Metek's mind was filled with many thoughts. He couldn't just lie, warm and snug, and wait—he must do something. He listened to his father's even breathing. Etah was sleeping soundly. Slowly he raised himself until he was sitting up, then he carefully climbed over the sleepers sprawled upon the floor. Fumbling about, he located his fur outfit and slipped into his parka and bearskin pantaloons. When he was fully dressed he placed his foxtail windbreaker between his teeth, took his harpoon and lance from the wall and crawled outside.

The wind had died down but the air was bitter cold. Metek moved along the snow wall of the house calling softly, "Karsuk! Karsuk!"

A mound of snow exploded and the big dog leaped out, shaking a shower of frost from his mane. He would have barked eagerly but Metek's mitten slapped the joyful greeting back into his throat.

"Quiet, big one," Metek hissed.

He dug the dog's harness from a hole in the snow where it had been hidden to keep the hungry brute from devouring it. Metek fastened the traces to his light sled. The sled had been built to be hauled by Karsuk alone. It was made of whalebone and walrus hide. To the sled was lashed the usual sleeping robe, stone lamp and a pot with a ball of moss and a bit of flint for fire-making inside its rock rim.

"We go to hunt," he said softly. "It may well be that the great light was sent as a sign. We may have meat when we return in the morning."

Karsuk growled and wagged his spring tail. A moment later they were off, Karsuk leaping ahead, whipping the sled across the snow, Metek running behind holding to the upright bar with one hand. His whip snapped out, first to the right and then to the left, never touching the upstanding ears of the dog, but always close enough to them to guide him. They raced down the slope to the shore and were soon running across the ice. Metek set his course along the shore. If he kept close to the ice rafts piled against the rocky beach he could see the dim outline of the cliffs and would not be lost.

On they raced, winding among the tumbled slabs of broken ice, skimming across smooth expanses that had been whipped clear of snow. They dropped into a valley formed by the crashing together of two massive floes and climbed out again over high ridges of crystal ice. Around them hung a great silence, and the stars were not able to banish the gloom, though the moon which circled without setting laid a pale glow over the world.

Metek watched and listened with keen senses. The only game he could expect to sight would be bear or fox, and there was a very slight chance that Karsuk might hear a seal under ice. If he met a bear the beast would be in a savage mood, lank with hunger and dangerous to attack. He had no idea how he would kill a bear with only one dog to help him, but he was a simple person and believed in strange things. He believed the aurora was a sign.

But the strongest urge was the desire to save Karsuk's life. He must hurry because he had taken the family supply of food away and he had not talked with his father before leaving.

The hours passed and he slowed his pace to a trot. The moon swung back in its endless circle and shed white light over the sea. He was well down the coast now, much farther than he had ever gone alone before. Ahead, lying low against the whiteness of the snow and ice, he sighted a rocky island a few miles from shore. Two hours later he was opposite the island. He knew he should turn back and deliver his dog to his father. But he kept going, hoping to sight a fox. He changed his course, crossing the wide channel to skirt the island.

At its far end he came to a rocky reef and beyond that there was a cove with cliff walls rising out of a mass of ice. Here was a good spot for fox. The little snow dogs liked the rocky cliffs. In the summertime they hunted lemmings and placed the fat mice down under the moss where the ground never thawed. In this time of hunger they would be looking for their caches of frozen lemmings. He trotted into the cove and followed along the base of the sheer walls. Halfway around the curving shore he halted and spoke to Karsuk.

"Easy, big one!"

The dog halted and stood still, his neck scruff rising, a snarl rumbling in his throat. Metek was staring at something he had never seen before. Two masts rose above a jumble of ice. Stripped of rigging, they rose naked and smooth like the barkless trunks of two trees. Metek had never seen a clipper ship, so he didn't know what the two tall poles were. He had never seen a tree with a trunk thicker through than the shaft of his lance. He didn't know that these bare, branchless trees meant that there, beneath the floe, in shallow water, lay the hulk of a whaler that had been driven by a gale into the arctic sea where it had been caught by the ice. In this year, 1750, the Arctic was an uncharted sea, which had been entered only by a few hardy adventurers whose ships had been frozen in and carried by the great drift into unknown regions where they were smashed when the floes came together.

Metek moved slowly toward the masts. He circled around them, edging closer until he was able to touch one of them. They were strange and wonderful things, growing out of the ice. Then he moved toward the sloping shore where the cliffs broke away. Here he came upon something more exciting and fearful than the masts. A crude hut stood against the cliff wall. Metek saw at once that it had been very lately occupied. Twice he moved away from it before he could gather the courage to creep to the doorway and peep inside.

When he did crawl up to it he saw that it had not been built by any of the Eskimo people. No Innuit ever had skins such as those tacked over this framework of ship's timbers. Metek ran his hands over the canvas wonderingly. Then he bent forward to examine the strange pots and other utensils scattered about. They certainly were not made of any stone he had ever seen. Two objects held his attention. A pair of Russian boots lay on the floor where they had been tossed aside. Metek touched one of them, then picked it up. It was a boot, all right, but of a strange design.

Metek backed away from the shelter and looked hastily about. He half expected the strangers to appear, but he saw no one, nor did he hear any sound. He was frightened, but his curiosity was too great; he wanted to see the men who had built this hut. Meanwhile, Karsuk had been growling and snarling—he mistrusted the scent left by the Creole Tartar sailors.

Then Metek moved on along the cliffs and rounded the reef. He faced toward the west, bearing a little south to keep the mainland in sight. He should turn back, but he wanted to catch a glimpse of the strange people. Day came with but little change in the light. The moon still circled overhead, shedding a pale light. Metek was tired and very hungry. Soon he must find a snowbank where he could burrow deep and rest. He saw no game at all, nor did he hear even the distant howling of the white wolves.

Finally he swung in toward shore. There seemed little use in staying out on the floe; he had seen no bear sign and no fox sign. Reaching the shore he moved along just outside the rough ice.

He was keeping a sharp watch for a deep bank of snow where he could dig a burrow. His pace was a slow, dragging walk now, and his stomach was knotted into a hard cramp that had stopped aching and was only numb and heavy. Suddenly Karsuk began growling low and warningly. Metek roused himself and leaped forward. He laid a hand upon the dog's neck and spoke in a low voice.

"Quiet."

If there was game ahead he did not intend to let Karsuk frighten it away. Karsuk stopped growling but his nose kept wrinkling and he was pointing directly toward a ridge of ice ahead.

Metek scrambled up the steep slope and crouched on

its top, peering down into the valley beyond. What he saw made him flatten himself against the ice. Three hunters were circling below. They had a she-bear cornered. Metek saw that they had killed her cub and that she was standing guard over the carcass. He shuddered, and pulled Karsuk down beside him. No Innuit would ever dare kill a cub before dispatching the old she-bear. The old she-bear would run away, but she would come back and kill the hunters.

The silence was suddenly shattered by two loud reports that echoed along the icy walls of the valley. Flames had leaped from weapons the men held in their hands. The hunters were at least fifty paces from the old bear, yet Ninoo, the wise one, tumbled over and lay kicking beside her dead cub.

Metek watched, trembling with fear and excitement, while the hunters rushed forward and fell upon the bear with gleaming knives. He would have whirled and crept away but the sight of bear meat held him—that and a great curiosity he could not understand. The magic lances of these hunters killed from a distance without throwing a spear or a harpoon. And they killed with fire, Metek had seen it leaping from the ends of the weapons.

A crack in the ice ridge allowed Metek to creep closer to the scene of the kill. Karsuk was quiet enough though his powerful body trembled as he pressed close against his master. Metek unhitched him from the sled and held firmly to his harness as they wiggled their way downward.

Poking his head up out of the crevice he watched the hunters. They were devouring slices of the fresh meat, wolfing the raw flesh ravenously. Metek's mouth watered and his numb stomach came to life enough to give him pain. The hunters were strange beings, their faces almost white in color, their features sharp, and their clothing different from any skins Metek had ever seen.

After a time, the hunters satisfied their hunger and began cutting slabs of meat from the carcass. They dressed
the cub and cut much of the better parts off the old bear.
One of them went off and returned with a crude sled.
They loaded the meat on the sled and lashed a canvas
over it. After they had piled on all they wanted, they
stood talking to one another. The strange words in which
they spoke seemed angry. Finally they caught hold of the
sled ropes and started off, quarreling loudly as they shuffled away.

Metek waited until they had disappeared, then he and
Karsuk leaped forward. They sprang upon the carcass and
Karsuk ripped pieces of meat from it, gulping them down
without chewing them. Metek was delighted to discover
that the white hunters had left the choicest parts of the
bear behind, the liver and the heart. He sat beside the carcass and pulled out his flint knife. Cutting the liver into
strips, he shoved them into his mouth, seasoning them
with squares of fat cut from the ribs.

Like all Innuits, Metek had a great capacity for food.
He did not move until he had devoured most of the liver.
When he could eat no more he began cutting slabs from
the carcass. He stripped the bones of all the meat he
thought Karsuk and he could haul; then he took the dog
and went after the sled.

When the sled was loaded, he found that he must
leave about half the meat behind. He felt sad because he
did not have a dog team to carry all the food back to the
village. At least he had enough for one big feast, and now
he must hurry because his people were hungry.

The big meal had restored his strength and he did not
tire for many miles. But at last he knew he must rest.
His muscles were aching and he was not making any head-

way. The wise thing to do was to sleep; then he could
travel faster. He would reach the village sooner that way.
He found a drift and burrowed into it. He could think of
nothing but sleep, and his eyelids drooped even before he
got Karsuk and the sleeping robe inside the shelter. Karsuk
would keep him warm and, by having the dog inside, he
thought drowsily, he would be sure the big fellow did
not tear the meat from the sled. Metek fitted a block of
snow into the opening through which they had crawled.
His burrow was now snug and tight. Within a few minutes
both boy and dog were asleep.

Metek was awakened by Karsuk. The dog was snarling
and barking furiously. Metek caught up his lance and
shoved aside the block of snow at the entrance. Poking his
head outside, he saw a huge form looming above his sled.
A gaunt white bear had scented the meat and was bent
upon taking it. Metek shouted angrily as he burst from
the snow with Karsuk close behind him. The bear was
savagely hungry and paid no attention to the boy. She
ripped the meat from the sled and was gulping it down
as fast as she could tear the frozen slabs apart.

Karsuk leaped at her and she whirled to lash out at
him. Metek jumped forward, his lance lifted. He drove
the slender shaft of bone and ivory straight at her heart,
heaving the weapon with all the force he could command.
The bear roared with rage and pain as the lance struck her.
She caught up the meat which was frozen into a solid mass
and started off at a run. Karsuk charged after her, lashing
at her hind legs and flanks, but he could not stop her.

A pack of dogs would have made her stand and fight;
one dog could not worry her enough to make her halt.
Her long snakelike neck with its rounded head swayed
back and forth as she galloped away.

Karsuk bounded in front of her and snapped at her face. She struck a sweeping blow and her massive paw caught him across the shoulder, sending him sailing through the air. He landed in a snowbank, with blood pouring from his shoulder, but he was not badly hurt. Being well-trained in bear hunting he had let his body go limp and the fall into the snow had done no harm.

Metek raced after the bear but he was soon left behind. He stopped running and plodded along listening to Karsuk's barking, which grew fainter and fainter as the bear raced on. Finally he sank down on a slab of ice to await the return of his dog. He had lost his lance and the meat he was hauling to the village.

Karsuk came back an hour later. He was battered and cut from the battle. He whined and rubbed his head against Metek's shoulder.

"The fault was not yours. I should have buried the meat," Metek said.

Then he sat down and began wondering what he should do. There was some of the bear meat left where the kill had been made, but it might be better to go on to the village and tell the hunters about the lone bear that had stolen his cache from the sled. The men could take her trail and kill her. If he went back after the remainder of the carcass he might find it gone. He got to his feet and led Karsuk to the overturned sled.

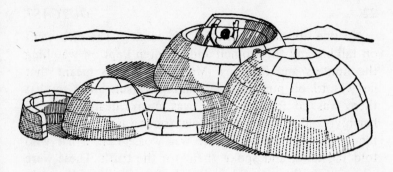

2. OUTCAST

Metek raced behind the sled while Karsuk bounded eagerly across the ice, his harsh yelp ringing back from the cliffs. They had rounded the point below the village and were starting to climb the slope. Metek was eager to spread news of the bear he had met. Karsuk scrambled over a pile of rough ice and the sled tipped over, bounced along, then righted itself as Metek grasped the upright bar.

No one was about in the village when they pulled up before Etah's hut. Metek unharnessed his dog and set the sled against the wall of the house. He buried the harness, then ducked down and scrambled along the passageway. Inside he could hear low voices talking. Pausing, he listened. The hunters were gathered with his father. That was fine, now all could hear his story at once.

Metek moved into the room. The hunters were seated upon the floor, their naked bodies gleaming in the light from the whale oil lamp. Beyond them, on the platform used as a bed, sat Metek's brothers and sisters and the children of Eiderduck huddled together so tightly they could not move. His mother and Eiderduck's wife sat on the floor beside the platform. The black eyes of the children were fixed upon the faces of the hunters. Metek saw at once that things were going very badly, that there had been no food for anyone since before he had gone away.

No one appeared to notice his coming. The men went on talking and the women and children kept on watching the hunters and listening. Metek knew this meant that he was to be punished for taking Karsuk away so that there was no food. A thief was always dealt with very harshly, and a thief who stole food was the worst offender of all. A food stealer was worse than a liar who told big tales, and spoke them for the truth. These were two sins the Innuits did not easily forgive.

Metek was not greatly worried. He began slipping out of his fur clothing. When he had removed the heavy garments he seated himself beside one of the hunters. Kablunth, the story-teller of the village, was speaking.

"We should go back, far into the hills, where Took-too of the big antlers has gone," he said.

Ugrang, who was old and very wise, shook his head. "Etah should take the dog and go out on the ice where the beast will scent the blowhole of Nutchook, the seal."

"We do not know that the dog has returned. Perhaps he has been hidden away so that we may not kill him," Kablunth said grimly. He did not look at Metek but the boy knew this was the beginning of words about him.

"I heard the dog return," Ugrang said.

Etah's father nodded. He had heard Karsuk's eager yelps while he was coming up the slope. But he did not agree with the old man.

"I say we must eat the dog, giving strong meat to the women and children, then we must go into the big hills and look for Took-too. If I go out on the ice I could only find one Nutchook and that would keep the evil one away no more than a few days." Etah looked across at Kablunth for approval of his plan.

Kablunth nodded his head gravely, then Kodloo, seated beside Metek, began speaking. He was short and broad-shouldered with a scar across his cheek put there by Ninoo, a white bear he had once challenged single-handed, and had killed with his lance. He spoke without looking at Metek. Not once had he noticed the boy.

"We must eat the dog and then hunt in the hills."

Then Ugrang, the old one, said, "We will hunt in the big hills and today we will find meat."

Kablunth agreed that they would have luck that day. Being the story-teller he was as near a medicine man as the village had. He was allowed to tell big stories and was not punished for making them up. He gave advice and knew many cures for sickness. Now he rubbed his hands up and down on his bare knees and closed his eyes. He spoke softly.

"Last night a dream came to my house. The spirits from the land of sunshine and warmth led many Took-too down a grassy hill to a great river. On the banks of the river were the hunters. There were many antlered ones slain and there was a great feast. It is a good sign. It may well be that Lito, the scouting one, will come soon with news of Took-too."

Metek waited impatiently. He dared not break into the deliberations of the hunters. He must wait until they had finished. When the story-teller finished speaking the men nodded and some of them smiled as they thought of the summer scene he had dreamed about. They had finished; all was decided.

"I saw many strange things." Metek spoke out boldly.

Only his father looked at him when he spoke and Etah's eyes were piercing, warning Metek to keep silent. He was not pleased that his son should speak out when he was awaiting punishment, but Metek went on in spite of the warning glance.

"I traveled far down the coast to where a rocky island stands off the shore. There I saw two great trees of bare wood growing out of the ice. On the shore I found a hut that was like no hut ever seen before. In the hut were many strange things."

The hunters did not move, but their faces froze into hard lines and their eyes gleamed with anger. The son of Etah was a food thief and to that crime he added the sin of lying. He had taken away a dog that was marked for food; now he was speaking big tales. Metek felt the chill of their disbelief, but he rushed on. He realized he had made a bad start, but he wanted to tell everything.

"Then I went past the island and came upon three strange hunters. They were attacking Ninoo. They killed the great bear with lances that flamed fire and they killed from far away but I saw no arrow or harpoon fly through the air. When I crept close I saw that their faces were white, almost as white as the snow. They talked in words I could not understand." Metek paused and looked around the circle of faces. None among the hunters believed him. Not even his father believed. He hurried on, eager to convince them.

"The hunters left part of the meat and I ate much of it, and Karsuk ate. We placed as much upon the sled as we could pull over the ice."

Kablunth lifted his eyes to Metek's face. "Then why did you not toss the meat on the floor so that all might eat?" His voice was harsh and cold.

"I grew very weary and made a burrow in the snow. While I slept a great bear came and made off with the meat from the sled. I wounded her so that she drags my lance with her. If you will go with me Karsuk will take the trail and you may kill her"—Metek spoke very slowly—"and if we meet the hunters we might trade fur clothing, which they do not have, for one of their magic lances. With such a magic lance we could kill game easily and there would be no hunger."

Kablunth laughed harshly. "There is no lance that kills with fire and no hunter could have a white face. If these strange men had no fur clothing they would stand naked and would freeze into ice." Kablunth looked at Etah and shook his head sadly. He was a little worried, but would not show it. This boy was imagining things which even he had never put into his stories. It would be well to have the boy banished or he might become a better story-teller than Kablunth himself. "I am very sorry, Etah, that you have a son who steals food, and lies," he said softly.

The others said nothing. One by one they got up and slipped into their fur clothing, then left the hut. Kablunth was the last to go. He paused before getting down on his hands and knees to crawl into the passageway.

"Today we hunt in the high hills," he said. Then, with a dark look at Metek, he disappeared.

When he was gone Metek and Etah sat for a long time in silence. The children looked at their brother out of big eyes filled with fear. They were suddenly afraid of him. His mother, alone, looked at him with tenderness in her eyes. She knew how well Metek loved his dog, and she was sure he had told the big tales to save Karsuk from death, and this did not seem so black a sin to her. At last Etah spoke.

"You have brought sadness upon my house," he said, speaking very slowly. "For the sake of all and mostly for your own sake you must leave the village. Never again will any man look upon you with favor or treat you as one of the people. No woman will look at you. There will be no wife for you among the people."

Metek felt a surge of anger rising within him. He had spoken the truth and for that he was to be driven out of the tribe.

"I will go down the coast to the village of Eiber," he said. "I would not stay."

"The dog will be left. We must have him for meat," Etah said.

"The village of Eiber is a long way." His mother spoke for the first time. "It is best that you wait until summer and go in your kayak upon the water."

"I go at once," Metek said stubbornly. "Perhaps I shall meet the white hunters and they will give me one of their magic lances; then I will return."

"You will have no meat to take with you," his father warned. "You may stay here in the hut, but it is best that you do not go out among the people. While you are here few will come to sit with us."

"I go at once," Metek said. He did not think about the hundred miles of bleak coast line to be covered before he could reach the four huts known as Eiber, where a dozen villagers lived. "I will pull my sled and take my sleeping robe, my lamp and my harpoon."

Etah did not argue or try to dissuade him. Metek dressed and followed his father outside. He would have lingered to speak with his mother, but that would have been childish, and he was now a man. When he stepped into the cold air Karsuk leaped up against him and tried to lick his face.

"Down, big one," Metek said softly. "Today we part." He shoved the dog away and turned to his sled. His father had not paused; he was striding toward the hut of Kablunth where the hunters were gathered.

Metek's preparations for departure were easy. His sled was already loaded and all he needed to do was to ice the runners. He did this by squatting upon the snow and filling his mouth with it. When the snow changed to water he squirted it upon the runners where it instantly froze into

a glassy surface. Rising from beside the sled, he caught
Karsuk by the scruff of the neck and shoved him into
the passageway.

"Get back inside," he ordered sternly.

Karsuk scrambled down the tunnel to the warmth of
the hut. Swiftly Metek turned and slipped into the sled
harness. He broke into a quick trot, heading down to the
sea. He had a simple plan in his head. First he would
locate the bear kill and take any meat that was left. Next
he would pick up the trail of the hunters and follow it.
Without a glance back, he ran on until the glow of the
ice tables closed around him and the village vanished.

Still cold favored him, with no wind, and he was able
to travel without halting. Hour after hour he swung along
until he began to grow tired, then he slowed his pace to a
dogtrot and finally settled into a steady walk. He would
keep going as long as the weather favored him. When the
gales came, he would have time to rest.

Reaching the island, he swung around it and headed toward the valley where the hunters had slain Ninoo. He
topped a ridge and looked down into the icy basin. The
depths below were flooded with moonlight, and the silence
was so deep he could feel it pressing down upon him.
Hunger had begun gnawing inside him so that he ran as
he descended into the basin. His eyes darted ahead eager
to sight the carcass frozen hard as ivory and good for his
need.

He located the spot of the kill and halted to look upon
the ice. He saw fox tracks and the great pad marks of
Ninoo, but there was no meat, not even a bone. He got
down on his hands and knees and examined the tracks. He
had a feeling the old bear he had wounded had taken his
back track which had led her to the meat. He peered
about. Perhaps the old bear was sleeping near by. He

finally decided that not enough meat had been left by the foxes to make Ninoo sleepy. Had she found enough to gorge her great belly, she would not have crushed the bones and devoured them.

For a half hour he searched for the sled tracks made by the white hunters. A gale had lashed the ice fields and swept away all traces of the trail. Metek seated himself on a slab of ice to consider his course. Days of travel lay ahead and he had no food to carry him along. Fear would have filled any white hunter with panic, but Metek was a child of the barren iceland. Like the little snow-dog, like Ninoo and Took-too, he had always lived close to such dangers. He got to his feet and stood listening.

There was a movement in the upper air, a stirring that he could hear. The wind was coming. A gust struck him full in the face and he slipped the foxtail muffler between his teeth to protect his face. Another gust broke around him and the air was filled with the roar of the gale. The wind drove the bitter cold through his clothes, chilling him at once. There was nothing to do but burrow into a snowbank and go to sleep.

Ducking his head, he moved toward a wall of up-ended ice. Here the wind was broken and a great drift lay piled against the slab of ice. He dropped to his hands and knees and began digging a tunnel three feet wide by four feet high. This he drove back six feet into the drift. He cut a block of snow to fit the opening. When the burrow was finished Metek pulled his bed robe inside, then buried his sled to keep stray bears or foxes from devouring the leather straps and the walrus hide which was stretched between its runners. He took the harness inside with him, plugged the hole he had used as a door, and lay down. He had nothing to cook so he did not light his lamp. Rolling up in his robe, he lay still.

The temperature outside the hut was sixty degrees below, inside the hut it stood at zero, a full thirty-two degrees below freezing. Had there been several hunters or even Karsuk inside the little room the warmth of their bodies would have made it fairly comfortable. The heavy robe kept out most of the chill but Metek did not sleep well. At intervals he awoke and beat his feet and arms to warm them.

In this manner he spent fifteen hours while the gale raged outside and piled the snow deeper over his hut. The gnawing hunger inside him kept growing until his stomach caved in and became numb. In the bitter cold his body needed fats and meat to keep up heat and to furnish energy. Several times he poked a hole with his harpoon and listened to the wind. At last he heard no rushing roar outside. The storm was over and he could travel again.

He cut his way out of the hut and he stood in the moonlight listening and looking about him. He would not run this time. His knees felt weak and his vision had become clouded, as it often does when a man is overtired and starving. Digging his sled from a drift, he loaded it and slipped into the dog harness. When he started, he headed toward the shore. He must find food, a fox or an arctic hare, and the most likely place to locate them would be near the cliffs.

Metek moved at a steady stride, leaning against the sled harness. He had made one, perhaps a dozen paces, when he heard a sound behind him. Whirling, he leaped to the sled and slipped his harpoon from its place on top of the bed robe. Across a drift charged a wolf. Metek gripped the harpoon and set himself to drive it into the oncoming beast. Yellow eyes gleamed and white fangs showed above and below a red tongue as the brute leaped upon him. Then Metek's harpoon clattered to the ice and he sprang forward.

"Karsuk!"

The great dog was upon him, leaping up against him, yelping and whining. They sank down upon the ice and the boy's arms closed around the neck of his dog.

"You slipped away and followed my trail," he said softly. "But you should not have come; you should have stayed."

When the first surge of joy over having Karsuk alive and safe had passed, Metek considered what he should do. He would be accused of stealing the dog again if he did not take him back. Yet he was so far from his home and he was not supposed to return. Furthermore, he had no meat to give as a peace-offering.

Karsuk freed himself and bounded about yelping and barking. Metek smiled. He slipped the harness upon the dog, then he got out his whip and snapped it in the cold air.

"We go on together. It is to be that way or you would not have found me."

Karsuk plunged forward and Metek caught the upright bar as the sled whipped past. The eager strength of the dog as compared to his own weariness gave him an idea. Karsuk must have eaten well before leaving the village. As he considered this angle, Metek grinned widely.

"The hunters brought meat and there was a feast. The scout brought news of Took-too soon after I left so you were not killed," he said, speaking to the dog. After that he felt better and ran after the sled with more strength.

They reached the shore and turned south along the rocky beach, keeping close to the foot of the cliffs. Low hills sloped evenly back to the base of a chain of mountains. On the south slopes Metek could see scrub timber sticking up out of the snow. His black eyes flickered eagerly. This was the country where the arctic hare lived. He

moved up beside Karsuk and slowed their pace to a noiseless walk while he scanned the gullies and hillsides where
the tips of the bushes showed.

His eager search was rewarded as they topped the third
hill. He saw a white shadow moving over the snow. Halting, he tied Karsuk to the upright bar of the sled.

"Stay there," he ordered sternly.

Karsuk lay down. His tail wagged and his eyes gleamed,
but he remained curled up while Metek trotted away.

Circling the hillside, Metek approached the spot where
he had seen the moving shadow. He came up with the wind
in his favor and a high bank of snow serving as a screen.
Carefully he thrust his head above the bank.

The big bunny was hopping along, his nose twitching as
he sought twigs sticking above the snow. Metek remained
motionless, waiting. The hare settled down and began
champing upon a frozen twig, biting off the bark and nib-
bling it, then chewing the twig itself. He was fat and the
stark hunger that filled every other thing in the bleak
wasteland had not seemed to worry him. Metek's fingers
tightened upon his harpoon. If he tossed the weapon he
might miss and put the tantalizing meal to flight. It was
best that he stalk the hare as a fox would.

Edging along the bank, he waited, his stomach urging
him to charge down upon the feeding bunny. The hare finished the twig he was champing. He had cut it off close to
the snow. His ears flopped forward and his nose twitched;
then he hopped away. With the stealth of a white wolf
Metek moved along the snowbank. The hare halted and
Metek halted. For a long space the big fellow sat looking
at the ridge as though considering the desirability of strik-
ing off on a long run up the mountain. Metek gripped his
harpoon. If the hare set off up the slope he must take a
chance shot at him.

The hare sniffed about, seated himself in a most awkward position, and thumped away at the side of his head with one furry foot. Having dislodged the flea which was biting him, he hopped into a crevice out of sight. Swiftly Metek moved forward on hands and knees, keeping his lips parted so that his breath made no sound. At the edge of the crevice he dropped to his belly and peered over the edge. The hare was seated with his back to Metek, nibling a twig.

Metek gathered himself together like a big cat. His harpoon was shoved aside and his hands slipped out of his mittens. For a long moment he poised, easing his weight forward, gathering his legs under him, then he leaped. He plunged upon the hare before the bunny knew he was in danger. With bare hands and eager teeth Metek made sure of his meal. The hare kicked and flopped, but Metek was taking no chances of losing his dinner. His teeth found the neck of the big one while his hands gripped the legs. With the body dangling before him he scrambled backwards out of the crevice.

There was no time or need for building a fire. Metek was in need of food. Quickly he stripped the skin from the carcass. His stone knife passed twice across the body and the hare was dressed. The skin and entrails were piled neatly. Along with the large bones, they would furnish a very scant meal for Karsuk. Then Metek feasted. In true Innuit fashion he did not stop eating until the hare had disappeared and the blood specks, frozen hard, had been gathered from the snow and devoured as dessert. Gathering up the skin, he trotted down the slope.

Karsuk bolted his share without pausing to chew even the bones, giving each a crunch before he gulped them down. Metek laughed as he looked up at the circling moon. The round tightness of his stomach gave him a feeling of independence. He was able to take care of himself. He had devoured more meat than any but an Eskimo could have stowed away and he felt strong, able to run fast again.

The miles slipped away and the moon reached the far edge of its circle, then swung back. Metek slowed his pace to a trot and allowed Karsuk to help him a bit when they came to rough ice. He kept a sharp watch for traces of the white hunters. He had a feeling they had headed south and east along the coast. He saw no sign at all, but a feeling persisted that they were ahead of him.

3. EIBER VILLAGE

The coast line swerved south and a shallow bay appeared ahead. Metek could see a jutting headland beyond and decided to cut across, instead of following the shore. The going was smooth for a time, then became rough, with ice piled ahead like rocks closely packed together and strewn over a plain in great heaps and endless ridges, leaving scarcely a foot of level surface.

Metek moved up beside Karsuk and they picked their way slowly, climbing sometimes ten, sometimes a hundred, feet above the surface ice where they could not go around the peaks. The spaces between the ice masses were filled to some extent with drifted snow. The sled wound through the tangled wilderness of broken ice tables. Metek pushed and Karsuk pulled. They struggled up to the summits of lofty steeps and then plunged down the far side, shooting along, with the sled bouncing and often rolling over.

After two hours of going they came to a high barrier. Climbing to its top, Metek halted to catch his breath. Another ridge lay within a few yards of the first with a snow bridge between. The crust was smooth and hard.

Catching hold upon Karsuk's harness Metek moved out on the smooth snow. He had only taken two steps when the crust cracked and gave way hurtling them down into a deep crevice. The space had been bridged by the drifting snow without filling the space between the walls of ice. Snow poured upon them as they wallowed about in the darkness.

Digging out of the smothering mass, Metek righted the sled. When he looked up he saw, fifteen or twenty feet above his head, the ragged hole where they had broken through. The walls were sheer faces of ice on the right and on the left and there was a real danger of the whole ceiling's crashing in and burying them completely. An uneven crack extended in both directions from the gap above and snow was sifting down as the crusted roof settled.

Metek moved along the crevice and found that it narrowed like a tunnel ahead of him. As he crawled forward, he came upon an object lying half-buried in snow. Examining it with his hands, he discovered it was a sled, turned upside down. His eyes were now accustomed to the gloom and he bent over it, his breath hissing softly between his teeth. It was the white hunters' sled. Metek sat down and stared ahead. It was possible that the men were still trapped in the tunnel. For a minute he was afraid to move on for fear he would come upon them. Then his panic left him and he started to walk, crouching over, listening, peering ahead.

Within ten feet, he came to a slab of ice which lay on a slant across the crevice. Climbing upon it, he worked his way upward and came to a jagged opening in the snow. The hunters had broken through and had escaped. Metek crawled through the hole and helped Karsuk drag the sled out. When he stood in the open again he looked around him. It seemed strange to him that these men should have abandoned their sled which had their sleeping robes and other necessary implements strapped to it. They could not hope to survive long without those things.

He looked about for their trail but the wind had swept it away so that he could not tell which way they had gone. After a brief study, he moved on down into a deep valley. The ridge he had just crossed proved to be the last of the rough ice. The jutting headland was less than a half mile away and he set off at a trot. As soon as he rounded the point, he began looking for a place to dig into a drift to rest a few hours. Locating a bank, he dug a hut and crawled inside with Karsuk. They snuggled close together, both yawned widely, and Karsuk went to sleep at once. Metek lay awake for a while thinking about the white hunters and wondering if he would come upon them. But he could not keep his eyes open long. He was a child of the wild country and fear and worry did not prey upon him when his stomach was full and he was tired. The rabbit meal had banished his hunger and it would not return for some time. With a drowsy yawn, he fell asleep.

Eight hours later Metek was awakened by Karsuk. The dog had finished his sleep and wanted to get outside. He sat up and patted Karsuk's head.

"We go far today, perhaps we will come to Eiber village before we stop," he said.

They were soon on their way, running strongly. Metek was not hungry. Like the wolf or the wolverine, he gorged when there was meat to eat, but could go for days without food when there was none. Even so, he kept a keen watch for foxes or hares. He must take game when he came upon it.

They ran on, mile after mile, without seeing a sign of life, hearing nothing at all, the glow of the reflected light showing them the way. Late in the day Karsuk sighted a fox and ran away with the sled. He would have taken the little snow-dog but for the drag of the sled. Metek raced after him, shouting encouragement, but the fox scrambled into a crack in the ice and hid well back under a berg. Metek could hear him snarling defiance and barking deeply under the ice. It would take most of a day to dig the little one out of his den, and Metek was not hungry enough to make the effort. Nor did he wish to lie in hiding for three or four hours, waiting to pounce upon the fox when he ventured outside.

They ran on and Metek began to wonder if they would be able to reach the village without resting again. Kablunth had said it was built on a jutting spit of sand where a big river joined the sea. Eagerly Metek watched for the spit and the river but he saw only rows of cliffs ahead.

Soon the cliffs gave way to sloping shores that rolled smoothly up to round foothills. Dimly Metek could see white mountains rising above the hills. The mountains seemed to beckon to him. He had a great desire to climb up to their gleaming peaks. But he kept on along the shore until he came to a place where the uplands rose out of the tumbled ice itself. Then he moved inland and traveled over low ridges and into little valleys.

A change in the weather came as he moved along. The air grew warmer until it was almost balmy and soft. Metek slowed his pace and shoved his hood back. He halted where a pile of boulders thrust round forms above the snow, and seated himself. Karsuk curled up, his red tongue lolling over his white fangs.

As Metek sat drinking in the mellow air he saw a movement among the rocks. Like a bump on the big boulder he remained still, not moving a muscle. Karsuk had closed his eyes and was asleep. A little snow-dog had emerged from his nest under a rock. He stretched, yawned very widely, then examined a bump in the snow and decorated it with a few drops of musk. His yellow eyes blinked as he looked all around, seeking any enemy that might be lurking near by.

Metek did not move. He hoped Karsuk would not waken until the white fox was far enough away from his burrow so that he could not whisk back into it. Here was a meal and the Innuit boy meant to have it. The snow-dog sniffed and trotted a few yards, not with the breeze—that would have been dangerous—nor against it—that would have added to his labor—but angling so that the least whiff of food would be carried to him. Metek's eyes snapped. The wise one was moving away from his haven of safety. Still he did not move, for he was very comfortable and not desperately hungry. The urge to kill any wild thing he saw was not in Metek. Unlike white men, he killed only for food or for the need of skins and never had a lust to destroy an animal just because he came upon it. He was always curious about wild things and liked to watch them.

The little white dog seemed to know that mother sea had nothing in her cupboard for him, so he did not head that way. He had just come from the floes, where he had followed a white bear for days, yapping at a safe distance, rushing in to snatch scraps when the larger animal made a kill, trusting his swift heels to save him from the ice-king's wrath. But hunting had been very poor for the great Ninoo and the little fox had deserted his huge comrade, remembering this valley where during the summer he had laid neat rows of lemmings in storage under the shallow-thawed earth, well down on the ice. Those little arctic mice would be fresh and fine. All he need do would be to search out one of his summer caches.

Even though he failed to locate one of his cupboards he would find some birch and willow browse to fill his little belly. He paused and sniffed, scratching at the wind-hammered snow. Down under that coating of armor were many live lemmings but they would be hard to get at, well protected by the crust and lively, even in the icy world beneath the snow. His best bet was to locate one of his storehouses where there would be one or two square meals. He had made a score of those caches, and one or two square meals a week are all anyone needs, at least so the snow-dog believed.

Finding a cache was no easy matter and the fox circled about, never moving far from where Metek sat. The landscape had changed with the coming of the howling blizzards and the deep drifts but the general landmarks were the same. This was the spot or at any rate this was the tiny valley where he had been so successful in catching lemmings the summer before. Too, the musk drops he had carefully placed about the cupboard would not be entirely removed. He sniffed about eagerly, wrinkling his little nose.

Suddenly he halted and thrust his nose into a crack in the crust. Here was the place; he was sure of it. He began digging with all the energy in his famine-lank body. Down he went, making a hole in the crust, tossing the snow up in a shower behind him. After the crust there was a space of loose snow, then the harder packed layer underneath which was near to the ice. At last he reached the frozen ground which required both fang and claw to penetrate it. Now the white dog was digging furiously because the luscious mice were within smelling distance, close under his nose.

Metek shifted and slid his harpoon forward. This was his chance to secure meat that would carry him on toward the village of Eiber. Then he froze to stillness. He saw another fox moving out of a pile of rocks close to the hole where the first one was digging.

The snow-dog in the hole was warned by his sensitive ears that someone was approaching. Instantly he was out of the hole and on guard. He knew that this was dangerous country, that bears and wolves might be roaming about, hungry and savage. In a moment he saw that no monster was near. But there, not three hops away from him, sat another little snow-dog, and a hungry visitor, too. But the fat lemmings down in the hole belonged to him, so he curled up his black snout and wrinkled his white face, exposing his sharp teeth. Then he growled as fiercely as he could and arched his back. He was giving the number two snow-dog warning that advance would cost him an awful price.

Number two moved forward slowly, a snow bump like the other. Then the owner of the cache seemed to recognize in the other an old acquaintance. They drew closer together and both lifted their tails, at the bases, flinging musk odor on the air. That is the law and each carefully obeyed it. Then they both grinned for now they were sure they knew each other. In fact the newcomer was a female and the last summer's mate of the little dog. They had drifted far apart since the joyous summer with its abundance of food. Savage hunger had driven them both back to this silent valley where they had labored together to store food.

The cache was really common property but most of the lemmings had been stored by the he-dog. He warned her back, then slid down into the hole and began digging furiously. She seated herself on the snow and sat watching, her yellow eyes flaming eagerly. And now there was a fine supply of meat close before Metek, yet he dared not move because the she-dog was facing him and would give a warning.

Down in the hole the snow fox had unearthed a row of lemmings fresh and good because they had been laid away on ice, and were frozen hard. Immediately he began a fine feast. When he was half full he allowed his mate to shoulder in beside him and they set about finishing the banquet.

This was the chance Metek needed. Both snow-dogs were busy down in the hole. He slid from the boulder and crouched forward. Before he could take a step, Karsuk awoke. He jumped to his feet with a low growl as the scent of the foxes came to him, a growl which was deep and carried instantly to the pair down in the hole. Like a flash of white snow caught up by the wind the little dogs leaped out of the hole. The she-dog darted toward the burrow where she had slept and her mate followed.

Karsuk charged after them and came to a halt with his muzzle thrust against a rock. The snow-dogs were down under a great boulder where they could yap and snarl at their enemy. And their little bellies were tight and full so they would lie down and sleep for a long time before venturing outside again.

Metek laughed softly. He was not angry with Karsuk and he was not greatly disappointed because the little ones had escaped.

"You are clumsy, big one, now the little ones laugh at you," he said.

Karsuk barked savagely and tore crusted snow away from the opening. He thrust his nose inside, then jerked it back as the he-dog snapped at him. Metek walked to the hole where the lemmings had been buried.

"Here are three fat mice," he said.

Karsuk slid into the hole and gulped down the three lemmings. The titbits made him feel better and he was grinning widely as he came up out of the snow. Metek hitched him to the sled again and they went on. The balmy air cooled and snapping frost made it clear and sharp again. Metek quickened his pace to keep his body warm.

A few hours later they came to a break in the rolling hills and the shore line below them turned abruptly north. Below, a low point jutted out into the sea. Climbing to the top of a rise, Metek saw the frozen expanse of a river's mouth.

This must be the location of Eiber village. Now they must find the huts of the villagers. As they moved down upon the level ground Metek examined every drift and pile of snow, seeking an opening that would be a doorway. At last he came upon a rounded drift that had a hole at its base. Rushing forward he shouted loudly. Karsuk barked eagerly, but there was no answer. Bending down, Metek examined the opening leading to the passageway which would have a room at its far end. Snow lay drifted deep against the doorway. The villagers had not ventured outside since the last storm, which must mean they had a supply of meat inside.

He got down and crawled into the passageway. There darkness met him and he moved forward slowly with Karsuk crawling behind him. Coming out into musty darkness he halted. There was no glowing kotluck with a sixteen-inch flame wavering under it to light the hut. And the damp chill told him the place was deserted.

Backing out, he searched for another hut and located two more whose entrances were not buried in the snow. Each hut was deserted. The villagers, following Eskimo custom, had decided to move when hunting became poor and famine visited the village. Metek knew there was no telling where they had gone, a hundred miles, perhaps, possibly to the village he had just left.

Returning to the first hut, he entered, dragging his belongings in with him. He made a fire and lighted his lamp. When the flame glowed enough to light the hut, he saw the former dwellers had left a kotluck and that there was oil in it. He lighted it and sat down on the floor to wait for the flame to warm the house. Karsuk growled as he seated himself beside his master.

"We are alone, big one," Metek said. "We will need food very soon, and oil to keep us warm."

Karsuk growled again. He did not seem pleased with the smells clinging to the deserted hut. Metek leaned forward and patted his head. Perhaps the dog smelled strange people—it might be the white hunters had paused here on their way south. He roused himself.

"Tomorrow we must hunt," he said. "And we shall watch for the white hunters." He knew that if they were to live until spring came with its days of plenty they must find game.

4. TOOK-TOO

Metek did not burn his lamp very long. He was not sure when he would make a kill which would furnish him fat to replenish it with. Lying down on the hard floor of the hut, he rolled up in his sleeping bag and soon fell asleep with Karsuk close beside him.

Anyone but an Innuit would have been deeply worried at finding the village deserted. Metek was alone with only his dog for company and months would pass before the sun warmed the land enough to banish the ice and free the river and sea. The villagers were not likely to return before spring. But that did not bother Metek much. Like the little arctic fox he did not worry until he became hungry. Later he would be lonely but now he was tired and sleepy.

Twelve hours later Metek was awakened by Karsuk. The dog had been outside the hut and had returned to see why his master was not up and hunting. Karsuk was always hungry and at that moment he was hungrier than he had been for a long time. His share of the rabbit had been very small. Metek sat up and peered through the deep gloom at his dog, then he grinned.

44

"You are hungry, big one." He pressed a hand against his own stomach. "I am hungry, too, so we will hunt."

He slipped into his parka and hood, which he had removed when he rolled up in the robe. Outside he found a still cold with the moon and the stars lighting the world with a half glow. Metek stood for some time looking up at the high hills. Barren ground caribou migrate in the winter, heading south in great herds, but a few always stay behind to defy the cold and the storms. If any had remained they would be in the high hills where the ridges were swept bare and the lichens and moss were not buried very deep. There was the sea, of course, and if he found no game in the hills he would travel out on the ice where Karsuk might scent the blowhole of a seal. Then there was the little valley where he had watched the snow-dogs. If he failed to locate Took-too he would return by way of that valley and try for fox.

So that he would be able to bring a supply of meat back and also have his sleeping robe in case he was caught in a blow, he took the sled. Karsuk did not like this idea very much but he struck out on a run. They swept across the flat delta and headed out upon the frozen surface of the river.

When they were halfway across the river Karsuk swerved and leaped a few yards to the right, then planted his feet and began snarling and yelping. Metek pushed forward and stood looking about. He saw nothing except a pile of drifted snow such as a log would have made. Karsuk nosed close to the drift and began digging. With his harpoon Metek broke the crust and shoved the snow away.

A seaman's cloth coat came into view and Metek started back. Karsuk would have leaped upon the form buried in the snow but Metek ordered him back. Slowly he edged forward and began uncovering the body. When he had fin-

ished, he knelt beside the dead Cossack. The man was one
of those he had seen far back along the coast. He bent and
slipped the Cossack's knife from his belt. It was a long
knife with a curving blade, sharper than any knife he had
ever seen before.

Metek had none of the fear of the dead which makes
some Indians rush in terror from the presence of a corpse.
The white-faced one's spirit had long since passed over to
the land of sunshine and eternal warmth. He would no
longer need his knife.

He made his way back to the river bank and then headed
toward the high hills. A very nearly full moon cast a flood
of glittering light over the ridges and rounded hilltops
ahead of and above him. Every crag and spire gleamed cold
and lifeless. The scene was desolate and mysterious; the
world seemed like a part of creation unfinished. To Metek
it was a familiar world and he moved upward at a fast trot,
following the ridges which skirted valleys filled with blue-
black shadows.

At last they came to a peak where the wind had whipped
the snow away, stripping the barren ground and exposing moss and lichens to the bitter frost. Below lay the sea,
cloaked in an ashen atmosphere. This was the place to
find Took-too, if any of the reindeer had remained in
the bitter cold of the far north. Metek seated himself with
Karsuk at his feet. He listened intently. There was no
sound, save the snapping of a rock under the stress of
the frost. Getting to his feet, he moved on up the ridge.

Now the ocean had vanished into the gray floor of the
vast abyss below. The wind blew steadily, but not with the
fierceness of a gale. Metek took the sheltered side of the
rise and kept going, deeper into the round hills, straight
toward the high mountains which rose like glittering cas-
tles of ice above him.

He came to a little mesa which was sheltered from the wind by a wall of towering rimrock. The snow lay several feet deep upon this flat meadow. Beneath the snow in a spot like this, facing south and east, Metek knew that there would be much cured grass, warmed by last summer's sun. Halting, he bent down and listened, his black eyes scanning the expanse of whiteness. Presently he heard a steady champing, like the clicking of little stones tapped together. His breath hissed over his teeth and then escaped quickly. That sound was the clicking of the teeth of a barren ground caribou. Metek peered ahead but he could not locate the beast.

Listening for a long time, he decided that there was only one Took-too feeding. Probably most of the deer's body was down in a pit he had dug to get to the grass. Metek slipped off a mitten and took from inside his parka two round stones. Then he laid a hand on Karsuk's collar.

"We will go back, big one, where you can be safely fastened," he said.

They moved back to the base of the high cliffs where he fastened Karsuk securely to a projecting rock.

"Down! Stay here!" he ordered sternly. Karsuk curled up beside the sled. He was disappointed because he was not to join the hunt, but he had learned to obey his master.

Metek turned back to the meadow and back-tracked to the spot where he had first heard the champing. After listening several minutes, he heard the sound again. Seating himself in the snow he clicked the two stones together. Then he listened. The deer went on champing grass. Metek clicked the stones again, this time louder. The champing ceased and Metek heard a deep grunt. His prey was a big bull, probably a lone patriarch who preferred the savage struggle with the cold and the snow to the long trek south.

Metek moved forward a few yards, then halted to listen. The antlered one was feeding again. The stones clicked steadily for a few seconds. Again the deer grunted, and Metek knew he was becoming interested. Took-too is an inquisitive beast and a silly one. He will investigate anything he sees or hears which is not actually chasing him. Metek knew that the caribou would eventually come to investigate.

After a half hour of clicking and waiting, Metek sighted the deer. The brute seemed all antlers as he moved across the snow. He had located the source of the strange clicking sound and had sighted Metek sitting in the snow. His capers were comical as he circled and doubled and moved ever nearer. Metek flattened himself on his face, digging down into the snow so that he was hidden. He kept the stones clicking away, but his right hand gripped his harpoon and he lay on his other side so as to have free use of that arm.

The caribou came on, stamping and shaking his head, jumping up and down stiff-legged. Now he had ceased circling and was moving in a straight line toward the hollow where Metek lay. The usual method used by Metek's people was to have two men in the hunt. One of them sat where the Took-too could see him, back on the trail a short distance; the other lay in the pit and waited, hidden from sight. The reindeer would walk up on the hidden man and could be lanced from close range. Metek was alone and had to take chances. The big one might become frightened and leap away before he was close enough for the kill.

Took-too came on, slowly now, with his head thrust out, sniffing and shaking his antlers. Metek clicked the stones softly and his chilled fingers gripped the shaft of the harpoon. The caribou halted ten paces from the pit and stared out of big eyes. Metek clicked the stones very softly. The reindeer shook his head and moved forward. He had seen nothing so far but the strange clicking came from the snow and he must find out what it was.

The big fellow's general appearance was yellowish-white in color, with his back a dark umber-gray. His throat fringe was pure white and there was a white ring around his eyes. His muzzle was caribou-brown, but his face was gray and looked, in the moonlight, like that of a solemn old man whose head had been sprinkled with fine snow. He took the last few strides to the edge of the shallow pit very quickly. As he loomed above Metek, his muzzle thrust out, the hunter shot his harpoon upward and forward, heaving all the weight of his body behind it, leaping to his feet with a shout. The ivory point drove deep. With a savage grunt the great beast sprang to the side and high into the air. He whirled and made off at a lope.

Metek did not charge after him at once, but wheeled and raced to where he had tied Karsuk. He found the dog pawing and jerking in a wild attempt to free himself. Quickly he slipped the harness from Karsuk and boy and dog tore away across the snow with Karsuk bounding a-head, leaving Metek far behind.

Very soon he heard the dog barking savagely and knew that Karsuk had come up with the wounded caribou. Increasing his speed he raced to the spot. He found Karsuk tearing at the carcass of the fallen deer. The big fellow was dead. Though his charge had carried him a half mile, Metek's aim had been true and his harpoon had done its work.

Then Metek learned the advantages and the superiority of the white man's knife. The steel blade cut cleanly and swiftly. He was so pleased with it that he paused many times to gaze at its shining edge. But tasting of his kill was of major importance now. Even admiration for the white man's weapon could not delay that.

First he cut several large pieces of meat for Karsuk. After that was done he opened the carcass and secured the liver and several strips of fat. For most of an hour he stuffed himself with strips of liver and bits of fat, filling his mouth until it would hold no more, then cutting the strip off close to his lips, and munching happily.

He finished his meal by eating a very ample amount of the paunch material. It had a sorrel, acid flavor and made a delicious frozen salad, because the bitter cold had solidified it while he was eating liver. No human stomach could digest the grass, lichens and moss as they are found in their natural state, but after the acids of the caribou paunch have partially broken them up, they become very fine and very digestible food. Thus Metek had his salad, the only sort of green food an Innuit can get in the wintertime.

With his stomach bursting, Metek started the job of cutting up the carcass. Having eaten many times the amount of food any other person, except an Eskimo, could have consumed, he felt lazy and inclined to lie down and sleep, but he knew the meat must be cared for. Finding this lone bull was much a matter of luck, and there might not be another within many miles of the spot. If he lay down and slept, the white wolves or a bear or the little snow-dogs might come and devour his prize.

He cut the carcass into large pieces, and, taking Karsuk, who was also ready for a long sleep, his shaggy belly distended with venison, went to get the sled. Several trips had to be made before all of the meat and the paunch were piled in a deep hole in a snowbank which lay against the wall of the cliff. Metek made sure of the safety of his cache by digging a sleeping burrow so close to the pile of meat that only a four-inch wall of snow separated him from it. He was sure Karsuk would hear any marauders who tried to break into his cupboard. With his bed robe spread, he repaired his harpoon, lashing the ivory blade to the shaft where it had been sprung when the caribou went down. Then he curled up, with Karsuk lying close against him, and went to sleep.

Metek was wakened by Karsuk's barking and growling. The dog had his nose thrust against the block of snow which filled the opening. His neck scruff was bristling and he was greatly excited. Metek opened a hole and peered outside. The moonlight shone on a number of grayish-white forms. Nine white wolves sat in a circle around the face of the drift. Their yellow eyes flamed and their white fangs gleamed. Metek knew they had come upon his trail and had devoured the bits left from his kill. He was sure they had not been outside his snow doorway very long or they would have started tearing the drift away to get at his cache of meat. He spoke to Karsuk.

"Down, big one. If you go outside they will kill you and carry you away."

Metek had seen the white wolves kill dogs many times. Big as Karsuk was, he would stand no chance against the arctic bandits outside. They would tear him to bits and devour him in a few minutes. Yet they did not look savage as they sat on the snow waiting for the leader's signal. They looked, rather, like large, gray dogs. One of them got to his feet. He sniffed about. Thrusting his nose into Metek's tracks, he wagged his tail and grinned widely, his red tongue lolling out over his fangs. Then he lifted his muzzle and bayed long and loud. The others took up the chorus and the cliffs rang with their eager, savage howling.

Karsuk would have joined the howling but Metek quieted him with a sharp slap. He did not want to excite the wolves. They might dig him and his dog out of their hideaway. He pulled his harpoon forward and loosened the shining knife at his side, then he made the hole bigger, so that he could thrust his head and shoulders through.

One of the wolves had moved close to the snowbank where Metek had covered the meat. He tested the snow and growled, then deposited a few drops of scent on it. After that he began digging. The others closed in, forming a circle around their leader, watching his every move, their black muzzles thrust forward, eager grins on their faces. They were lean and gaunt from their battle against the white famine which held the land, but this was their way of life. During the summer they feasted and their bellies were always full. They ate and they slept. But during the dark winter they fought against hunger and cold. Why they had not gone south on the heels of the great caribou herds, was something no one could understand. Perhaps it was the same instinct that had made the Took-too bull remain to challenge the terrors of the long night. Many of them stayed, and all grew lean and hungry, with death by starvation weeding out their packs.

Metek thrust his harpoon forward. He wrapped the seal-hide line around his arm as he thrust. The point and the barb sank into the shoulder of the nearest wolf. Instantly he leaped back, snarling and snapping at the unexpected pain that had struck him. The line tightened and the wolf threw himself over in the snow, kicking and biting. The others jumped back and stood watching.

Slowly Metek pulled the big fellow toward the opening. When the wolf was close, Metek thrust at him with the long knife. The blade drove deep and the wolf sprang backward again, jerking the barb of the harpoon free. He bounded away, swaying and staggering over the snow, leaving a crimson trail. Twenty paces from the hut he fell and slid across the crust.

The smell of hot blood drove the pack to a frenzy. They

were not bound together by any leadership but that of the wounded wolf who had been the strongest and most savage of them all. They had not been long together, only drawn into a group by the smell of Metek's kill. Now they pushed forward and fell upon their wounded comrade. With howls and slashing and snarling they devoured the carcass, dragging the bones away to crush them.

Metek thrust his head and shoulders out of the dugout. He shouted loudly and waved his harpoon. The wolves faced him, their yellow eyes staring at him curiously. They connected him with the killing of one of their number and they had a strange feeling toward this human animal which was different from any feeling they had toward any other creature. The white wolves had met Eskimos before, and had found that man was the one animal who seldom ran from them, and they were more prone to attack a fleeing foe than a facing one. They were fond of the flesh of sled dogs, but killed them only when they could raid a team without having to face the lances of the Innuits. Although they were curious about Metek, they did not fear him just because he was a man—that fear would come later, to their descendants, when guns invaded the far north and men came who would kill wild things because they were wild and for very little reason other than that.

Metek realized that he had the advantage, now that the wolves knew they were facing an armed man, yet he could not let Karsuk get outside. The big dog would attack the wolves and be killed. No dog lived who could handle even one wolf in an open fight. He kept on shouting, hoping their hunger had been lessened by the meat they had devoured.

The white ones seated themselves upon the snow and stared at Metek, who continued to shout and wave his harpoon. The wolves kept watching him. Finally one of them

got to his feet and moved a little closer. The others followed and formed a new crescent, sitting down casually,
with tongues lolling. Metek went on shouting, but the
wolves seemed unafraid. Again they moved closer, and now
they were all within easy range of the harpoon's long strip
of seal thong. Metek took careful aim and hurled his
weapon. The ivory blade found its mark and another white
one pranced about, struggling to free himself from a sudden
terror that had fastened upon him.

This was enough to convince the pack that their quarry
was dangerous. They bounded away across the snow while
Metek scrambled outside to finish the wolf with his knife.
He did not get a chance, for the big fellow had pulled free
and made away. Metek shouted at Karsuk who had started
after the wolf. Karsuk came back because he knew the
danger of following a wolf away from camp and being
trapped by the pack. This time the wolves did not set
upon the wounded one, but seated themselves on high
points and howled dismally at the moon.

Metek did not go back to his bed. He dug out his sled
and loaded it with all the venison he and Karsuk could
haul. The remainder he buried deeply, though he had little hope of finding it when he came back. No snow cache
would keep the white killers from stealing his food. They
would come as soon as he left and dig it out.

With the sled ready, they struck off across the little
flat. The wolves watched them go, but they did not follow;
instead they contented themselves with howling and yelping at the moon. Metek moved on down the slope, across
rounded hills, following ridges where he could.

After a time he could see the bergs and the spires which
filled the frozen sea. In a few hours he would get back to
the huts, where he could make a hot fire in a kotluck and
take off his heavy clothing. He was descending the white

expanse of the last hill when the wind sprang up. Within a
few minutes it was roaring in from the ice-filled ocean,
driving the loose snow ahead of it, biting through his clothing with a thousand needles of frost.

The distance was so short that Metek decided to brave
the cold in an attempt to reach the village. He lowered his
head and moved on amid a swirl of flying snow. The moon
was now a dull glow of yellow light shining upon the
smother of fine ice that rode the wind.

Metek's pace was slowed, but he did not stop. He wanted to reach the warm hut. If he burrowed into a bank now
he might have to lie chilled and uncomfortable for many
hours. Karsuk's bristling coat was hoary with snow and
frost but he strained against the harness straps while Metek
pushed at the back of the sled. Numb of body, with hands
and feet aching from the cold, Metek finally stumbled
across the flat shore and pulled up before the deserted hut.
He unloaded the sled and dragged the meat inside. The
temperature in the hut was lower than outside, but there
was no wind. Metek beat his hands until they ceased to
ache, then set about making a fire.

When the kotluck was glowing and the hut was filled
with heat and yellow light, he feasted in true Innuit fashion. He could not call in friends to sit with him and chip
frozen meat from the saddle of venison he had set before
him, but he kept a steady stream of luscious food pouring
into his mouth until he could eat no more. Then he sat for
a time staring at the wavering, smoking flame. The warmth
made him sleepy and he rolled up in his bed robe.

Like the white wolf or the fox or the bear he would
sleep, now that his stomach was again filled. Karsuk had
eaten, too, and was asleep before his master put out the
flame in the kotluck.

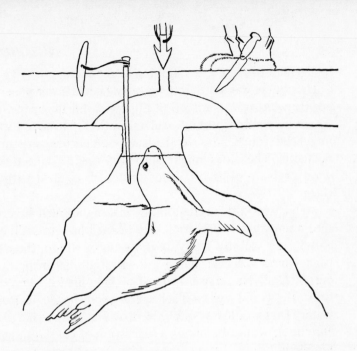

5. NUTCHOOK

Metek stayed close to the village as long as his venison lasted, making only short trips, a mile or so in extent. These trips were exploration tours made in the hope that he could locate either the two white hunters he had not found with the dead Cossack or evidences of the direction they had taken in leaving the region. He found no traces of them but his thoughts kept returning to them and his resolve to learn the secret of their magic weapon so that he might return with it to his people grew stronger. One day he returned to his venison cache, and found it had been robbed by the wolves.

For two days after he and Karsuk had picked the last scrap of meat from the rib bones of the caribou Metek remained at the hut. Being an Innuit, he had not thought of doing any serious hunting as long as the meat lasted. Now that it was gone, he prepared to set out. This time he decided to try the sea, hoping to get a seal.

His course was south into country he had never penetrated. He went in this direction hoping to locate open water where he would find both seal and walrus. This open water might be found in several places, sometimes very unexpectedly. The floes might shift and open a lane due to wind pressure or the shifting of the whole field with the tides.

Metek was not worried about making a kill if he could find open water. His people had learned how to stalk Nutchook, the seal, by studying the ways of Ninoo, the white bear. Ninoo was considered the wisest animal living in the barren land. Ninoo went about making his kill very carefully. He would sight a black speck upon the ice near open water. That would be Nutchook drowsing at a resting place. Nutchook would be taking a succession of cat-naps, hardly ten seconds long, lifting his head between times to scan the ice fields and the sky. Ninoo would fling himself upon his side and creep along when the seal's head was down. The moment the seal's head came up and his big eyes darted sharply about, Ninoo would stop short and begin talking to the seal. In this talk he could make a noise very different from his ordinary voice. The seal would be charmed, suspecting no harm, and down would go his head for another nap. Ninoo would shuffle forward noiselessly. This would go on until Ninoo was near enough to the seal to leap upon him and strike him down.

Metek had heard Kablunth tell this story many times and believed every word of it. Kablunth always said that if the Innuit hunters could only talk as cleverly to Nutchook as Ninoo could they would take many more seals. The hunters imitated Ninoo as carefully as they could and Metek had learned the seal call and how to slide forward, to halt, and to deliver the triumphant thrust if the seal did not take alarm and dive into his hole or into the open water.

Twenty miles were covered before Metek thought of turning back. Then the weather softened a little and snow began to fall, blotting out all landmarks and making traveling on a given course impossible. Metek knew that soon a gale would whip the storm to a raging blizzard. He changed his course and began returning over the way he had been following.

The cold wind came and shelter had to be sought. Metek located a drift and made a hut. Crawling in, he spent a miserable night and day while the storm raged over his nest. When at last he crawled out to find the air still and cold, he was lank and gaunt, very hungry and very stiff from the chilling he had undergone. Karsuk was hungry, too, and eager to be off hunting.

It was not wise to go on along the shore seeking open water. If he did not find food soon he would not have the strength to get back to the warm hut. He must go back and rest in the snug shelter, then he could go out and hunt again. He would be weaker but better able to travel.

The snow was loose, with no hard crust, so that traveling was slow and required much strength. Metek had to push on the sled most of the time. He and Karsuk struggled along, making only a few miles each hour. The rest periods came oftener and Metek began to have a strong desire to lie down on the ice and close his eyes. He knew he must not do this, that he must not stop and make a hut or he might freeze to death.

The white drifts were very inviting. They looked soft and warm like a huge bed waiting for him to jump in. But Metek knew that if he lay down he would be so comfortable that he would not move. Then he would begin to dream pleasant dreams about a warm hut and a feast. He would go to sleep and he would never waken from that dream—it would go on and on and never end but he would be frozen into a block of ice which the white wolves would find and break apart.

Metek had seen hunters frozen into hard ice. When the rescue party located them, they were always smiling, thinking about the dream which had frozen inside their heads. And he had heard an old man, who had been found before the frost drove its ice needles through him, tell how the dream came and how pleasant it was.

So he kept plodding on with a little wind stinging his cheeks and the pale moon lighting his way and gleaming on the cliffs along the shore. But he had to pause to rest, standing behind the sled, holding fast to the upright bar. At last he knew he could not go much farther. He felt that he was walking fast, but he was barely moving; Karsuk was really pulling him along with the sled. Karsuk halted and Metek sank down beside the sled. He meant to get up right away and go on. The village was but a short distance away now. His head sagged forward and his eyes closed for a moment. They opened and he shook himself but he did not get up.

When his head went down the fourth time it stayed down. Metek was dreaming. He was back in his father's hut and they were having a feast. Etah had returned from a hunt bringing with him a portion of the carcasses of two deer. A general invitation to a feast had gone out and all who could crowd into the hut were there, their naked bodies gleaming in the yellow light. The women had been made to give up the bed and a deerskin had been spread to place the meat upon. There Etah did the carving. With a hatchet he peeled and peeled the sides. Chips of ice and bits of meat flew into the faces of the guests and were snatched up with much talk and laughter. As fast as frag-

ments of venison rolled off the men took them and reduced
them to sizes adapted for handling, using their seal knives.
The saddle was chopped up and divided, then the shell was
attacked, being split and broken into pieces. Everyone was
given a share and all began eating.

When Kablunth handed Metek's share to him he suddenly jerked it away again and shouted:

"Here is the liar, the teller of big tales who is also a
thief. He shall have no food!"

Metek grabbed for the meat but it was gone and he
felt cold wind on his face. He opened his eyes and Karsuk
was standing over him shaking him and growling. Then he
knew he had been dreaming and that if Karsuk had not
wakened him he would have started to eat the sweet meat.
He sat up and shook his head.

"Down, big one. It is no use. I can go no further."

Then he noticed that Karsuk was nosing into the snow
a few feet from the sled and growling softly. Metek crawled
forward. He was suddenly revived a little because he knew
Karsuk had discovered something. As he bent down he saw
that the dog had located the blowhole of a seal.

Down under the ice the seal had a tunnel up to the surface. The tunnel was perhaps ten feet long, the thickness
of the ice. At its top there would be a little igloo cut out
of the ice where the seal could lie and rest. In the dome of
the little igloo was the small hole Metek was staring at.
Through that hole the seal breathed, pressing his nose to
it at intervals. No doubt the beast had been alarmed by
Karsuk and dived down into the water, but he would come
back because he could not stay long in the water under the
ice. The wait might be long, but Metek made ready.

The first thing he did was to pull the sled close so he
could sit upon it. Next, he drove his harpoon down through
the snow and into the little hole, working it up and down

to make sure the shaft would slide when he thrust it downward. Then he prepared for a long, cold wait.

An hour passed and Metek began to grow drowsy again.
The cold was numbing him and fighting to make him sleep.
He shook his head and gritted his teeth. When Nutchook returned he must be alert and ready for a thrust. Twice he
nodded and wakened himself with an effort. Once he dozed
off and was awakened by Karsuk's warning growl. He
thrust the spear downward but hit nothing. The seal had
come and had gone.

When he was so numb he was sure he must give up, he
heard the welcome blowing of the seal as he caught a few
breaths of the chill air. Metek tensed his muscles and drove
the harpoon downward. He felt the blade strike and sing,
then the line payed out and he wrapped it around his
waist, twisting it tight. The seal hit the end of the line
and Metek was jerked upon his face, where he lay hanging
to the line, hoping the harpoon would hold.

The barb clung tightly and the struggles of the stricken
seal became weaker and weaker, until they finally ceased.
Metek made the line fast to the sled and set to work with
his knife, cutting a big hole in the roof of the igloo. This
was slow work because the ice was thick and very hard.
After two hours of working and resting, he had the hole
cut. The nearness of food kept him from getting sleepy
and banished his weakness. Then began the tug to get
the carcass out upon the ice. This took time but he finally
dragged the seal out of the hole.

Metek fell upon the fresh meat with his knife while
Karsuk worried a flipper, gnawing at it and gulping down
the bits he could tear away with his sharp teeth. In a few
minutes, Metek was feasting on warm liver, grinning broadly, all of his troubles forgotten. He did not move until he
had eaten a huge amount of food, then he pulled the seal

up on the sled and lashed it there. It could be dressed after they reached the hut.

The run to the village was now only a pleasure trip for Karsuk and his master. They trotted along, one pulling, the other pushing. Metek was sleepy but in a very different way. They reached the hut and Metek dragged the seal inside. After a fire had been made, he dressed the beast, laying aside a supply of fat for the fire-pot.

Metek ate some more choice pieces of seal, which he cooked over the wavering flame of the kotluck. His stomach was tight as a skin drum when he had finished, because it was already full before he ate the cooked morsels.

Lying upon his robe Metek stared up into the gloom. Karsuk lay beside him licking his paws and digging with his teeth into his thick fur. Metek let his sleepy thoughts wander back to his home village. When he returned they would have to make a big feast, because he would bring with him the magic weapon and the knife. He would have many tales to tell and when he got back from his travels to the south he would know more than Kablunth. He would be an even greater story-teller than Kablunth. He grinned sleepily, and with these thoughts filling him with a warm glow, he fell asleep.

6. THE SUN RETURNS

The days and weeks of half-light passed slowly. Metek was lonely, but he was not really homesick. He wandered far up and down the coast on hunting trips. Sometimes he was hungry, and sometimes gorged with food. When he was hungry he hunted and prowled with Karsuk ahead of him pulling the sled. When he had plenty of meat he ate and slept and dreamed within the warm hut.

February brought almost broad daylight for a few hours in the middle of the day. Metek could see far through the cold air. For the first time he looked upon the new country where he had been living. It was a different country from the Point Barrow region. The hills back from the shore were mountains and seemed very high to him. But the ocean was the same, an ice-locked expanse with bergs and rafts smashed together, all covered with gleaming snow.

Metek made a daily stand on a rocky promontory where he watched for the sun. Among the people there was no greater event than the return of the wanderer to the sky. Below the promontory, a lane of open water appeared as the great floes stirred and shifted. This lane extended far out to sea, a narrow ribbon of water which the spring winds would not let freeze over. With the open water came walrus, as though by some magic, and one day Metek saw a flock of speckled birds sheltering themselves under the lee of the ice-shore. They were *Dovekie,* and the sight of them made Metek jump up and down and shout. They sent their plaintive cries across the waste of ice. Metek did not try to catch any of them. He was too glad to see them and to hear their voices.

One day Metek sat on his lookout peering out across the expanse of ice. He was keeping his daily vigil, watching for the sun. The expanse of open water had spread until it was wide, like a great lagoon. Numerous bergs and rafts of ice were dotted over it, but otherwise it was nearly free from ice. On the rafts lay walrus and seals, riding the swells like shipwrecked mariners. The surface of the water was agitated by the winds which never ceased blowing, now that spring was coming. It was a vast, bubbling caldron, seething and foaming and emitting vapors. The curling streams of frost-vapor which rose over it sailed away on the wind toward the southwest, where they disappeared into a dark mist-bank. Little streams of young ice tinkled and crackled over the restless waters. To the south the high ridges rose, white, glistening, with the shore cliffs etched sharply against them. There was little change in the bitter cold, but there was light and the light played upon the clouds floating over the white ramparts of the mountains.

It was among these clouds that the first fire from the sun appeared. Metek stood with arms lifted, watching while the wanderer poured a stream of golden fire through the clouds, and the whole southern heavens were ablaze with the splendor of the coming day.

Presently a ray of light burst through the mist-bank hanging over the sea, blending the mist-clouds with the sea in a purple haze, and glistening upon the silvery spires of

the tall bergs. The ray swung nearer and nearer and the glittering spires multiplied, as one after another they burst into the blaze of daylight. Soon the cliffs behind Metek were glowing with warm color and the hills stood forth in new robes of brightness. And now the line of the shadow was in sight. Metek held his breath, waiting, his mouth open, ready to shout. There appeared upon the ice foot a sheet of sparkling gems and the sun burst broadly in his face. Metek's shout rang across the water and echoed back from the cliffs. Karsuk bounded about howling and yelping. The friend of all hope, the wanderer who brought summer and life to the bleak land had returned. Metek flung his arms wide and shouted the welcome of his people to the giver of warmth and plenty.

Had he been home in his native village, he would have raced to tell the news and there would have been wild celebrating and much feasting. For soon the glaciers and the great bergs would weep tears of joy, Took-too would skip and bound gleefully over the ridges, the ice would loose its iron grip upon the waters and let the wild waves roar in freedom. The birds would come, knowing the wanderer would give them moss beds for the nesting time. The flowers would bud and bloom. For all this the people would be wildly joyous because the white one who kills with hunger must retreat and the land become a place of bounty. Food would be plentiful and no one would be hungry.

Metek stood for a long time upon the rocky lookout. When the sun dipped into the ice fields again, he turned back to his hut. He must hunt once more because he had no meat. Months of bitter cold still lay ahead of him. The sun would not temper the air for a long time and winter would grip the coast until forced to leave. Metek decided to try to take a walrus. The fearsome and aggressive old

bulls were beyond his power, but he had sighted several
smaller animals and meant to try for one of them.

Returning to the hut, he made his harpoon ready and
fashioned a lance. A search of the other deserted huts had
provided an old shaft and Metek used his stone knife for a
head. He had the white man's knife, so he did not need his
own. The lance suited him after he had tied it in several
ways. Finding an implement to drive into the ice as a
stake to hold his line was a more difficult job, but at
last he located a length of ivory tusk and fastened a bone
handle to it. He was now ready for the dangerous sport of
attacking a walrus.

Metek fastened Karsuk inside the hut, lest the dog alarm
the beasts when he crawled up on them. He did not take
his sled but set off on foot at a fast trot. When he had
approached the open water as closely as he dared while
walking, he dropped to the ice and slid forward. The group
of walrus he selected were near a little cove formed by
the washing and beating of the waves against a great raft.
To the right of the walrus herd a dozen seals were resting,
sleeping and watching at intervals.

Creeping up behind a slab of ice, Metek peered over it.
Ten rather small beasts lay on the ice, watched over by a
huge bull. The bull was a full eighteen feet in length and
his square, blocked-out face, with its rounded muzzle and
lips masked by quill-like bristles, massed at the base of his
thirty-inch tusks of ivory, gave him a fierce expression.
His great size and the steep descent of his forehead took
away all that resemblance to man which often reminds the
hunter of his own kind when he watches the seal.

The bull, like any man, was very fond of his own voice,
and now he lay listening to himself. His song was something between the mooing of a cow and the deepest bay-
ing of a dog, very round and full, with the barks coming

quickly, repeated seven or eight times. As Metek edged forward the big bull slid into the water and the others followed him with a great splashing. They rose and sank at intervals breaking through the new ice along the edge of the cove with an explosive noise that could have been heard for miles. When the walrus was above water Metek lay flattened upon the ice, motionless, not a part of him moving. As soon as the round heads went down, Metek darted forward, tumbling into a hollow or sliding behind an ice bump when the smashing sound broke out again. Metek had selected a small animal well away from the old bull. He seemed to know how long this walrus would be down, as well as where he would come up again.

At last Metek reached a plate of thin ice barely strong enough to bear his weight, at the brink of the pool where the herd was playing. Metek was very excited as he uncoiled his line of many fathoms length. The free end of the line he looped around his neck while he drove the ivory spike into the ice. He was now ready for the real test of his prowess. Metek began uttering a cry that sounded much like the song of the old bull. The walrus he had selected, along with all the others, rose above the water, sending pieces of ice flying. They stared with solemn faces at Metek. Curiosity was great within them; they moved in toward the thin plate of ice.

The animal Metek had selected swerved and slid in nearer. Down he went, and when he came up he was close to the ice, almost beside the point of the harpoon. The beast, still very curious, rose breast high, shaking the water from his crest. He fixed one good look at the hunter before plunging. That long look cost him all that curiosity can cost. Metek hurled his harpoon, driving it into the right flipper. Instantly the walrus plunged and as quickly Metek slipped the line from around his neck and took what a sailor would call "double in a bight" upon the ivory spike driven into the ice.

As the walrus went down, Metek played out the line freely, pressing it down against the ice with his feet. Now the death struggle began, with victory for Metek depending upon his skill and the strength of his line as well as upon the temper of the other beasts in the water. The line was drawn tight one moment and the next it cut through the water as the beast charged about under the surface. Then there was a crashing of ice and two walruses broke through. One was the harpooned animal, the other a young female who seemed terribly angered because of the harm which had come to the male. Metek was glad he had selected a very small animal.

The wounded creature charged against the ice, bringing his tusks down upon it and smashing great pieces free. As it broke under his weight, his bark changed to a roar, and foam poured from his jaws. Metek thrust repeatedly with his lance until the beast plunged back into the water. The female continued to try to climb up on the ice, using her fore-flippers to pull her body upward. A stab from Metek's lance sent her diving away.

For two hours Metek fought to keep a tight line upon the plunging Awak and to drive home a mortal wound. The animal charged continually, tearing off large pieces of ice and refusing to retreat until he had received a new wound. But at last Awak began to weaken. He fastened upon the edge of the ice with his tusks and could not or would not loosen his grip. There he hung, glaring at Metek, bellowing savagely while the female circled and roared a few rods away.

Fortunately, the rest of the band had made off, with the giant bull leading them, so that Metek did not have to worry about a mass attack. He sat down to await the end, which came quickly, once the walrus had fastened himself to the ice.

And now the great task remained of getting the beast out of water. Had he been even a medium-sized animal Metek could never had landed him, but he was small, so there was a chance that the Innuit youth could haul the carcass upon the ice. He made two pairs of incisions upon the neck, where the hide is very thick, about six inches apart and parallel to each other, so as to form a couple of bands. The free line from his harpoon he slid through these bands, passing the line over an upright slab of ice and bringing it back through the lower band. The walrus blubber oiled the line and made it slip easily. This gave Metek a double purchase and he heaved with all his might. The carcass rose, slipped back, then rose again, and finally toppled forward upon the ice.

As usual Metek began cutting as fast as he could in order to feast. Quickly dressing the animal, he secured the liver. This was the part which should be eaten first because it was the best. The boy feasted for an hour, seasoning the liver with slices of raw blubber.

Eating the meat raw was more than just a result of a ravenous appetite demanding food, it was nature's way of protecting her children. With no green food or vegetables to be had in winter, Metek and his people would soon have contracted scurvy and many other dreaded diseases but for the eating of meat raw. Metek's people ate much cooked food but when they prepared themselves for a long, hard journey through the cold they did it on a course of frozen seal meat eaten raw.

Having eaten all he could, Metek cut off a large piece to carry to Karsuk. He set off at a trot so as to get back before Ninoo or a pack of white wolves stumbled upon his kill. As he approached the hut he heard the yelps of the

imprisoned dog, and when he pulled the ice block away
from the low passageway the big brute leaped out. Metek
tossed the chunk of walrus meat to him and Karsuk fell
upon it.

"I do not know how I shall take you to the south,"
Metek said, as he watched the dog devour his meal. "It
may be that you will stay here and wait for my return."

There was no great delay because of Karsuk's feeding.
The dog managed to swallow his portion of meat almost
whole. Then Metek harnessed him and they set off to bring
in a part of the walrus.

Within two hours Metek was back at the hut and had
stored away a fine supply of meat. The part he could not
haul he had cached by piling ice slabs upon it, hoping that
by shoveling snow over the hidden cupboard he could fool
the wolves and the bears.

Instead of going to the hut and curling up to sleep, he
wandered down to the frozen river and searched along the
shore, poking into the drifts with his lance. After a long
search he found what he sought, a light boat which had
been left there when winter came. Metek dug it out of the
snow and sat down to look it over. He intended to repair
it carefully and have it ready for use when the break-up
came. During the three months he must wait for open
water, he would sew and oil and strengthen the kayak for
the trip south along the coast.

The craft was a slender affair with a light framework of
bone and wood, its withes lashed together with sinews.
This frame had been covered by stretching wet sealskin
and sea-lion hide over it, the whole covering being lashed
and sewed tightly. In drying, the skins had contracted,
making the shell taut and rigid, like the parchment head of
a bass-drum. The top was covered except for a round hole
formed by a curved bone ring. This was the opening the

boatman sat in. The whole boat had been soaked many times with thick seal-oil which kept the water from penetrating the skins.

Metek dragged the kayak up to the hut and placed it on the roof. He would need a double-bladed paddle, which he might find by digging in the snow along the shore of the river. He must mend several rents in the sides and bottom and the skins needed oiling. But the kayak was a good one and Metek was delighted.

A great restlessness had come upon him. No longer was he continually faced by the grim specter of hunger. The open water had come and food was assured. He was lonely and wished to find others of his kind. Talking to Karsuk was not like talking to another hunter, even though Karsuk listened and always wagged his spring tail. Metek was sure the dog understood, but Karsuk could not talk. Metek could not keep thoughts of his home village out of his head. The feasting time had begun and his people would be making merry every night.

To quiet his restlessness he took long trips into the hills and out on the ice. He searched for traces of the white hunters, but never found any beyond the one lonely grave on the frozen river. He grimly put thoughts of return to the home village out of his mind. He would travel far south, farther than any of his people had ever gone. When he returned he would be a hero among the people.

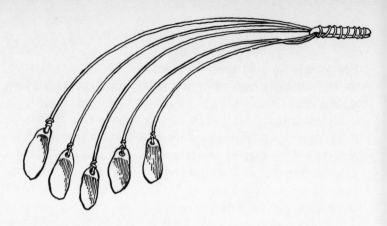

7. THE EIBER VILLAGERS

On a sunny day in late April the Eiber villagers came down
from the hills, running behind two dog teams. Their belongings were piled on the two sleds and the dozen nomads
trotted behind. Two strong men guided the racing dogs,
lashing out with their whips, shouting as they swept off
the brow of the hill above the village.

Metek was filled with wild joy as he heard them coming.
He leaped outside the hut with Karsuk beside him and
waved his arms. His shout was answered by the returning
wanderers. They came bounding out across the flat shore
and swept around him. Their dogs would have piled upon
Karsuk, who was willing enough to mix in battle with the
eleven savage huskies, but the men lashed them back,
shouting and laughing.

The hut Metek had been living in belonged to Noosha,
owner of the six-dog team and story-teller of the village.
Noosha had a wife and three children, but only one of the
family really held the attention of Metek. She was the
daughter of Noosha, and was called Lito. Her cheeks were
rosy and her lips red. Her fur parka was decorated with the
bills of little ducks and with shells. She stood back from
the others and looked at the stranger, her small, tapering

hands clasping each other.

"You have come out of the north and have stayed here during the cold and the darkness? " Noosha asked in a deep voice.

"I have been here long," Metek answered.

Atwa, the driver of the five-dog team, said, "You are a great hunter or you would have died of hunger. Now do you have meat for a feast?"

"I have meat," Metek answered. He had brought in a young seal that morning.

"Go. Get the fire ready in the hut," Noosha said to his wife.

Lito and her mother and the wife of Atwa and the children went into the hut to prepare the seal. The men remained outside talking. Atwa and Noosha told how they had gone back into the hills, to a valley where Took-too wintered. There they had hunted and no one had gone hungry. Noosha was curious as to why Metek had traveled so far in the dead of winter. Metek considered his answer carefully. He decided not to mention the white hunters. Perhaps later he would take them to where the Cossack sailor lay frozen. Noosha, he gathered, considered himself a great story-teller and might not like to have a boy outdo him.

Noosha gave him a very good out when he said, "Perhaps the young man has wandered far because no girl smiled upon him at home. Perhaps there was no girl in your village who was of the age."

Metek laughed and when he laughed both Noosha and Atwa were sure the story-teller had hit upon the truth. It was common custom among the Innuits for a young man to set out seeking another village when he had become a hunter.

Atwa said, with a wide smile, "You have come to the

right village, for Lito is full of smiles and dreams much about a hut of her own."

Noosha laughed and nodded his head. "I think you have come to the right village and now it is spring when the birds come mating and then everything in the world finds a chosen one to share in nesting."

Metek did not know what to say and was glad the talk was interrupted by the dogs. Wolf, the leader of the Eiber pack, had sought to settle matters with Karsuk. Wolf was a savage, hump-backed fellow who looked more like a hyena than a sled dog. His ears were frosted to stumps and his face was scarred by many battles. In Karsuk he scented a rival who must be soundly trounced and put in his place, or his supremacy might be challenged and another might get the best pieces of meat and the best mate.

The men stood watching, but made no move to stop the battle. The two dogs would have to settle their affairs or there would be no peace in the pack. As the two big fellows advanced upon each other the rest of the huskies stood back watching, their eyes flaming eagerly. They knew and hated Wolf, but they were afraid of him. If this stranger won, he would be no better than Wolf had been, so they would not side with either. They would wait and accept the winner.

Like a couple of king-wolves the two dogs advanced upon each other. Their tactics were those of the wolf. They did not leap upon each other, but moved in warily, feinting and watching for a chance to slash each other or to lunge and fasten upon a good hold.

Wolf leaped first and Karsuk met him, tossing him aside and slashing his shoulder. Again they advanced and again Wolf lunged. This time he was smashed to the snow and Karsuk was upon him. Howling and snarling they rolled over and over. Karsuk tossed Wolf from him and leaped in

again. He shook the big dog and hurled him to the snow
where he fastened upon his throat. Wolf kicked and lunged.
He flung his body over and twisted Karsuk's neck until the
big fellow had to loosen his hold.

Wolf knew he had met his master, but he made one
last charge. Both dogs went down, but Karsuk came up on
top and Wolf howled his surrender as he scrambled away
to join the pack.

The men laughed loudly, and Noosha shouted, "There is
a new leader of the pack. Now we will go inside and eat."

Metek followed his new friends into the hut. The kot-
lucks of the women flamed under the kolopsuts, or Innuit
baking dishes. On the floor lay the flipper quarter of the
last walrus Metek had killed. The women had selected this
instead of the fresh seal kill. They bent over the frozen
meat and cut it into steaks. Soon each kolopsut smoked
with a burden of fifteen pounds of meat. The men and the
children seated themselves and waited, their mouths watering, while the heated air of the hut grew heavy with the
smell of cooking meat.

Metek sat beside Noosha, but his eyes followed the
slender girl, Lito. She was not unmindful of his eyes but
she did not look at him as she spread a deerskin on the bed
platform. Soon the meat was cooked and the smoking
platters were set on the platform. Everyone crowded around
and gave full attention to eating. In a very short time all of
the meat had been eaten and the pots scraped for the last
drop of grease and fat. Lito sat beside her mother, but she
ate from the same bowl as Metek. Their heads bobbed together when they bent over the kolopsut and they both
laughed. Thus they became properly introduced, and were
shy of each other no more.

After the meal, the dwellers sat around while Noosha
led them in singing. Their voices were strong, but each sang

in his own key and used the two or three notes he liked best. The result was a lusty, inharmonious chorus. After the singing Noosha told a story, one of his best. Everyone listened intently, laughing where the story was amusing, and sighing where the great hunter suffered from hunger and cold. They all knew the story—even Metek had heard it many times—but they were as interested as though they were hearing it for the first time.

The heat inside the hut made clothing unnecessary, almost unbearable, so they all removed their garments except a few scant pieces. The yellow light gleamed upon their bronze skins like lamplight on a group of statues. After an hour or so of merry-making, everyone began to yawn widely. As there were only thirteen of them, counting Metek, they all curled up on the floor of the one hut, and upon the bed platform. Metek lay with his head against the broad back of Noosha. Noosha's baby daughter curled up inside his arm with her head upon her mother's arm. In a few minutes everyone was asleep.

Metek thought dreamily of how he had slipped out of his father's hut while everyone was sleeping just as the Eiber villagers were now sleeping beside him. For the first time since leaving home he considered abandoning his adventure trip to the south. Summer lay ahead, the time of glorious freedom and lazy ease, of hunting and fishing and playing. Lito would make a fine companion for trips into the hills or out on the surf. He yawned sleepily and closed his eyes.

So Metek dropped into the way of the people. He and Lito were together much. They watched life return to the bleak coast and to the river mouth. They sat long sunny hours on the rocky lookout stone, high on the promontory, and watched the ice grind and crash as it gave way before the sun and the wind.

And other birds came. Lito and Metek sighted the first pair. They were on the beach, running, with the wind blowing in their faces—racing along in answer to an urge to give their muscles play, to rejoice because the air was warm and soft. The birds, a pair of eider ducks, swept over the river's mouth in swift flight. They seemed undecided what rocky shore they would select for their summer home. Metek and Lito halted and stood, hand in hand, looking up at them. Lito waved as the pair flashed away into the sun.

"They are going home," she said softly.

"Yes," Metek answered.

"You and I, Metek, we are home," she said and laughed, then pulled her hand from his and raced away with her black hair flying in the wind.

Later that day they sighted a pair of graceful terns. The birds wheeled and swept down over the sea, screaming as they dipped into the white-capped waves.

The next day they saw burgomaster gulls in large numbers and a great cloud of little auks which descended upon the cliffs to rest before sweeping out to sea. Gerfalcons sailed about with solemn gravity as though feeling that they alone were delegated to keep a dignified manner while all the other wild things gave free expression to their delight. The air was filled with the shrill "ha-hah-wee-ee" of the long-tailed ducks.

Lito came running to where Metek was sitting on the sand. She was carrying Noosha's bird net.

"We will catch the little auks," she cried.

Metek jumped to his feet. He needed no second invitation; only the lack of a net had kept him from heading for the cliffs. His mouth had been watering ever since the first wave of little auks swept over the rocky point. He took the net from Lito.

"Shall we run?" he asked.

Lito did not answer. Already she was flying along the sand, headed toward the cliffs. Metek raced after her, the long-handled net over his shoulder.

Hundreds of little auks swarmed around the cliffs, which rose several hundred feet from the slopes on both sides of the river. Those hillsides were covered with loose rocks and boulders. The birds moved among the rocks, seeking the narrow, hidden places where they could lay their eggs and hatch their young. Little foxes scampered away as Metek and Lito approached. This was the time of feasting for the little snow-dogs and they made the most of it, gorging themselves upon eggs and young fowl.

The birds were very noisy, having just returned from the sea where they had been feeding. Metek and Lito moved up through the rocks until they were halfway up the slope. They crouched behind a boulder and watched the auks skimming along the slope. A constant stream of birds rushed over the hillside, flying only a few feet above the stones, and, after making their rapid flight the full length of the hill, they wheeled and swept higher into the air, sweeping back over and over again in the same formation. At intervals a hundred or so would drop down as though playing "follow the leader", and for an instant the whole slope for many yards would be swarmed with them, their black backs and pure white breasts making a gay design. Metek laid a hand on Lito's arm.

"You must lie down," he said softly.

Lito was much excited, so excited she had been standing up, and this caused the birds to fly out of reach of Metek's net. She dropped down behind the rock, but kept her head up so she could watch.

The birds swept lower, darting so close to the big rock that Lito could have reached up and touched their white breasts. An unusually large flock came sweeping along and

Metek got ready for the catch. Up went the net and a
half-dozen birds crashed into it. Stunned, they fluttered
and flopped while Metek quickly slid the long staff through
his hands and seized the net. With his left hand he pressed
down on the birds, while with his right he drew them out
one at a time, and, because he had only two hands, he used
his teeth to crush their heads.

Lito sat beside the rock catching the dying birds and
locking their wings across each other so they would not
flutter away. Metek spat blood and feathers from his mouth
as he worked the net, making haul after haul.

Finally Lito cried, "We have enough for everyone."

Metek put his net down and they sat side by side stripping the skins from the birds and eating the tender flesh
while it was still warm. Having eaten as much as they could,
they gathered up the remaining birds and started down the
hillside. Lito carried the net, while Metek carried the game.
She wandered in and out among the rocks seeking fresh
eggs which she placed in a bag tied around her waist.

That night the villagers feasted upon roasted auk,
cooked to a brown turn over a fire of driftwood coals.
They sat outside their new huts which had been erected
for the summer. These were the tents, which the Innuits
called *tupics,* fashioned of sewed skins and supported by
sticks. Big rocks were laid along the lower edges of the
skins to keep the wind from blowing them away.

Lito and the women, with the help of the children,
spent hours daily gathering down which the birds had
plucked from their breasts to make linings for their nests.
All bird skins were brought in and prepared by the women
into warm underclothing. The women sat on the sand and
chewed the skins until they were soft and pliable for weav-
ing. The making of a shirt was a long and very serious
business. As many as five hundred auk skins might be used

in making a garment ample enough for the burly form of
Noosha, whose wife was forever asking Metek to catch
more auks so that she might have the skins. Lito started a
shirt for Metek which caused much rivalry between mother
and daughter with Metek the butt of it all. If he gave skins
to Lito her mother would be angry and he did not wish to
have Lito's mother against him. He would have given all of
the skins to the girl but dared not deliver so much as one
to her while her mother was about. So he worked out a
simple plan. Each time he made a catch he brought a dozen
skins to Lito's mother and hid the rest under a flat rock
where Lito could find them.

Noosha enjoyed the troubles Metek got into and laughed
over them, using them in his stories, so that Metek would
flush and run away when the story-teller started on one of
his big tales.

But there was a great deal of fun when there was no
work to be done. Metek and Lito hunted eggs. They knew
that the eggs of the eider duck, like those of all ducks,
were strong and of poor flavor. But the eggs of the little
auk and those of many other birds were very fine and
they gathered many every day.

One day a visitor appeared at Eiber village. He paddled
up the river and beached his kayak close to where Metek
and Lito were fishing. When he saw Metek his face dark-
ened into a frown. Masumah had come from the village
above Point Barrow. He and Metek had hunted and fished
together. They had been rivals in all sports and games.
Being of the same age they had learned the craft of trailing
and surf-riding at the same time. Metek got to his feet.

"Greetings," he said.

Masumah did not answer, but his frown changed to a
scowl. He turned from Metek to Lito and spoke. As he
spoke he smiled widely.

"I have come to trade for dogs. We have none and wish to grow new teams." His eyes flickered toward Metek briefly. "Our last dog was stolen."

"Karsuk was not stolen. He followed after I had gone away," Metek said.

Lito looked from Metek to Masumah. She felt the tension between them.

"I will take you to my father," she said.

Masumah walked beside her as she headed toward the huts. Metek followed a few paces behind. He was greatly worried. Masumah might tell the villagers his story. If he did, Metek wanted to be there to tell his side of the tale.

Noosha and the others welcomed Masumah and the men seated themselves while the women prepared meat and fish for a feast. Karsuk walked up and sniffed at the visitor's boots, then growled and walked away. He had never liked Masumah very well.

Masumah waited until they had eaten their fill before he talked. Then he told the villagers about the famine that had come to the village and finished by relating how Metek had told lies and how he had taken Karsuk with him when the dog had been marked to be used as meat for the women and children.

Everyone listened in silence. Lito was seated beside her mother and her dark eyes crept to Metek's face as Masumah accused him. Noosha and Atwa remained grimly silent. After the visitor had ceased speaking, Metek broke in, eager to defend himself.

"I did not lie, nor did I steal the dog. He broke loose and followed my trail. He came up with me many miles from the village. I do not believe he was needed for food. I think Masumah is lying, because Karsuk was not starved when he came up with me." His eyes fastened upon his accuser and held there defiantly.

"Have you told these people about the trees growing out of the ice higher than hills and the white hunters who killed with fire-sticks?" Masumah asked angrily.

"I have not," Metek admitted. His hand slid inside his leather coat and came out holding the Cossack knife. He had never displayed that knife before. He now handed it to Noosha. "I came upon the dead body of one of the hunters, frozen upon the ice. I took this knife from him because he would not need it."

Masumah bent forward with the others. Noosha turned the knife over in his hand, then tested the blade with his teeth. Gravely he handed it to Atwa who tested it in a like manner. Then Noosha shook his head.

"I have seen a knife like this before," Noosha said slowly. "I once killed a sneaking Dog-rib hunter who carried such a knife." He stared hard at Metek as he added, "I did not keep the knife, but buried it in the earth, for it was evil. This is a Dog-rib knife."

For the second time in his life, Metek felt the chill of disbelief and cold anger settle over a group of friends. The Dog-rib people were not sea-hunters but mountain Indians. They hated the Innuits savagely and the Innuits hated them. Metek knew the white hunters were not Dog-ribs. He had seen the tall bony men of the Dog-rib tribe. Once he and his father had hidden on a mountain slope and watched a hunting party pass.

"The dead hunter was not a Dog-rib," he said, but as he spoke he knew his happy stay at Eiber village was over. He did not look at Lito for fear of what he would see in her eyes. But Masumah was looking at her, smiling in a friendly manner. The only answer anyone made to Metek's words came from Masumah.

"I have the right to take this dog, Karsuk, back with me. I would take two females and another male if you can

spare them. After the pups are able to run by themselves,
I will bring the dogs back."

"You have the right to the big one and we will let you
take two females and another male," Noosha said gravely.

Metek got to his feet. He knew there was nothing to be
gained by staying in the group. No one would speak to
him. He walked slowly down to the river and stood looking at the kayak Masumah had arrived in. His eyes flashed
as he recognized the boat. It was his own kayak. He had
built its frame, and his mother had sewed the sealskin and
walrus hide for it. Masumah had always been envious of
its slender lines and its speed. Even the paddle was his. He
sat down beside the kayak and stared at it moodily.

After a time Noosha came down and stood beside him.
Metek spoke to the older man.

"This is my kayak. I built it and my mother sewed the
skins. I will take it and keep it."

"Yes, that is what Masumah says," Noosha answered,
and having said what he came to say he turned about and
strode away.

Metek had forgotten about the trip south. Not in weeks
had it entered his head. Now he knew he would soon be
paddling away. He thought of Lito and knew that his re-
gret in leaving was because of her. Rising, he stood looking
up at the village. Lito and Masumah were walking across
the sand to where the dogs were quarreling over the bones
of a seal. Masumah was laughing and Lito was looking up
at him. Metek walked up the beach toward the tents. He
must secure his lance, harpoon, lamp and sleeping robe
from the tent of Noosha.

As he came out of the tent with his things, he saw that
Lito and Masumah were leading four dogs toward a rock
ledge. The children stared at Metek but the women turned
their faces away. He strode down to the shore. He stored

his things in the kayak, tossing Masumah's robe and spear upon the sand.

Getting into the boat, he laced his jacket tight around the hoop which circled the hole in the top. When he had made his craft water-tight, he reached down and caught up his paddle. Shoving the kayak off the sand, he drove the paddle deep into the water.

8. LONESOME SHORES

As Metek sent the kayak darting out into the current of the river, he looked back at the village. The people were gathered outside their tents watching him take his leave. Lito stood beside Masumah with her hands lifted, then suddenly she started running down to the beach, waving to him. Metek turned the boat about and sent it back to the landing. Lito waded out into the icy water and caught the edge of the kayak.

"Take me with you," she said. "I do not want to stay."

Metek looked up the sandy slope and saw Masumah and Noosha running toward him.

"Your father comes to take you back. But do not let Masumah carry you away to his village. I will come back and get you when I have things to prove I do not lie," Metek said.

"I know you do not lie or steal," Lito said and began crying softly.

Noosha waded out and caught the girl's arm. "Come," he said, and gave the kayak a push so that it moved out into the current. Then he shouted to Metek, "Go and do not come back!"

Metek dipped his paddle deep. He was angry and would have challenged Noosha but he had been taught that no

man can take a girl away without the consent of her father. She belongs to him as much as any of the things he
owns. Lito waved at him and Metek drove the slender
boat faster and faster.

As he rounded the cliffs where the lookout stones were
piled he saw Lito's mother shove her into a tent, then the
cliff wall shut out the village. Metek pointed the kayak
south and paddled hard, sweeping the blade downward
viciously. The shore slipped by as the kayak moved along,
mile after mile. Presently it flattened a little and became
low and slightly rolling with small sandstone and mud
cliffs at the sea's edge. Gray and brown in color, it showed
little patches of green where the snow had melted earlier
that spring. The course of the many streams which carried
away the melting snow were plainly marked over the dreary
tundra by dark fringes of dwarfed willows, alders and
birches which grew only along their banks.

On and on Metek drove his frail craft, unmindful of the
seas which swept in, roaring against the low cliffs. He was
in a great hurry to get to the end of his journey, though he
had no idea where he was going or how far.

Late that day he landed upon a cheerless beach of mud
and pebbles. There was an inlet on his right and low cliffs
where many birds swarmed. He seated himself and began
cutting a square of sealskin into strips to make a net.
Fashioning a bow out of willow and a handle out of alder,
he lashed the strips to the bow, then knotted them to
form a basket-like net. Within an hour he had caught
enough birds to make an evening meal. To the meat he
added a half dozen fresh eggs which he found along the
shore of a marsh.

That night he slept soundly, though there was no darkness. In the morning he was up and after eggs for break-
fast before even the birds had stirred from their rookeries.

Having eaten, he headed southward again, moving at a swift pace. The shore did not change much as he drove along. It was bleak and lonely, a scarred line, gouged and torn and battered by the onslaught of the winter ice. This was not promising or cheerful. If this land to the south was all dead and dreary he would find no living beings.

But Metek would not turn back. He believed that if he kept going he would come to the land of the white hunters because the lore of the Innuits said that there was no land beyond the great frozen sea except the shore upon which they lived. That shore, so went the tales of the old men, reached far into strange lands. Though the flat desolation seemed endless Metek was sure it would change. But when his course shifted and the coast line turned due west he was worried deeply.

The end of his westward voyage came when he sighted two remarkable promontories. The southwestern one, rising abruptly from the surf, was covered with loose, gray stones and barren of vegetation. The northeastern one rose gradually, and, although thinly covered with verdure, it formed a pleasing contrast to the gray head of the other. This double-headed cape rose a thousand feet above the sea. Metek had come to a great landmark on the Alaskan coast, Cape Lisburne.

Passing around the cliffs, Metek found that his course was again due south and he pushed on without running the foaming surf that pounded at the bases of the promontories. The valleys running back from the coast line were greener here, and the hills were higher and less worn.

Far below the two headlands, just beyond on a rocky point, he sighted dwellings which looked from the sea like the huts of Innuits. As he rounded the point and turned into a wide harbor, which was really the mouth of a river, he saw many people on the rocky shore, and many boats lying on the beach. Metek sent his kayak darting in toward the beach.

A pack of savage dogs discovered him and came howling down to the edge of the water. The dogs were followed by a crowd of children. The older people stood looking at him. Metek had never seen so many people in one village before. He stopped paddling and let his craft float a safe distance from the shore. Now that he was close he was not so sure about these people. The tufted thatches of their huts were covered with slabs of angular clink-stones from the beach and many racks stood about with fish drying on them. This was not as it would have been in the villages to the north.

A dozen men came down to the beach and beat the dogs back. They stood smiling and beckoning to Metek. He dipped his paddle and slid in close to the shore. As he unlaced his jacket from the ring in his boat they crowded close and when they started talking Metek knew they were Innuits.

They were curious about him and wanted to know how far he had come and where he was going. When he said he was going far to the south they shook their heads. Many savage and warlike people lived along the coast. There were many friendly hunters, but others killed Innuits upon sight. Metek gathered that these killers were like the Dogribs. The people told him that many days' travel would take him in a great circle around a rocky coast along the shores of a windswept sound, after which he would travel westward again until he came to fast water racing between their land and another lying to the west.

The fish the people were drying were the salmon with which the neighboring waters teemed. The women were busily cutting the fish and hanging them to dry so that a strong smell of fish hung over the village. Metek looked upon these people with wonder. The children ran about almost naked, pendants rattling from ears, nose and lower lip. The young men of Metek's age wore narrow bands of fur around their heads, into which they had stuck eagle and hawk feathers. The noses of the older men bristled with porcupine quills and bits of polished bone which had been inserted through the dividing wall of the nose. The men had more hair on their faces than was common among Metek's people and many wore heavy mustaches. Their clothing was different, too, the parka of both the women and men being made from the skins of ground-squirrels, and ornamented with the tails of the rodents.

Everyone welcomed Metek and the women set out a feast for the men. He was given the place of honor before a big stone bowl. This bowl contained a delicacy of which the people were very fond. It was Metek's first acquaintance with a fruit of any kind. The women had gathered red raspberries. The berries had been prepared by saturating them with rancid fish oil and pressing them into cakes. When dry the cakes had been broken up and tossed into the bowl which was well filled with oil. All the feasters dipped into the bowl and stuffed the mixture into their mouths eagerly. Metek ate some of the berries, but he did not care for the taste of the strong, rank oil, though the tart flavor of the fruit was good. He liked the dried fish and ate a great deal of it.

After the feast was over a large part of their catch of salmon had disappeared into the stomachs of the villagers, who had appetites as big as those of Metek's people. Then the men sat around talking. They told Metek he had arrived just in time to join in the great festival called "drowning little bladders in the sea". Metek was much interested and promised to remain for the ceremony.

That night he slept in the hut of a hunter who had a birchbark boat with a sail. This man was from the Innuit

village at the mouth of the great river. Metek guessed from
the hunter's talk that he had made the long and dangerous
journey north to settle at the northern edge of the salmon
run because he had done something, perhaps as grave a
crime as Metek had committed. He had brought to this
northern village many of the things his own people
enjoyed. The birchbark boat was the wonder of all, and so
was the sail. Because of it, he was deemed the greatest of
all the people and it was his privilege to offer his hut to a
visitor.

That night Metek was visited by a great many small
creatures that infested the hunter's house. They attacked
Metek and he could not sleep for scratching and fighting
them. At home he had known vermin but his mother had
always hung his clothing over the kotluck at night, heating and smoking the little ones out of the fur. These
people seemed to pay no attention to the little ones. The
hunter and his wife and children slept soundly.

The next day Metek joined the villagers in their festival.
He had never seen a great ceremony and everything seemed
very wonderful. To him the crowd assembled was indeed a
multitude. A hundred bladders, taken from animals killed
only with arrows, had been tied to a strip of skin which
was supported by poles driven into the ground. On these
bladders had been painted fantastic figures. At one end
of the kasga, which was a large hut used as a meeting place,
hung a large owl with a man's head and a gull's carved from
wood; at the other end hung two partridges. By means of
a string run over the beams of the ceiling, these figures
were made to dance and move in a lifelike manner. Below
the bladders, near the floor, was placed a stick six feet in
length bound around with straw.

Metek sat on the floor with a number of other young
men and watched every move that was made. To him the

figures and the bladders seemed really alive. One of the older men danced before the bladders. Twice around and back again he whirled, lifting his knees high, swinging his head. Then he bent and pulled a straw from the stick, and, lighting it, passed it under the bladders and birds so that the smoke rose around them. He then caught up the stick and carried it outside chanting and talking to the sea spirit, Ug-iak.

All of the people began to dance before the bladders as soon as the stick had been removed. They danced in the meeting house and outside. Metek could not help joining them and was soon singing as loud as he could and stamping about as though he had always lived among these people. The dance lasted all day and at evening the people gathered around their fires for a big feast.

That night Metek slept outside, telling the great hunter that this was the way his people always slept. He heated his bed robe over the fire and let the smoke chase away the little ones, and he did the same with his clothing, so that he slept well that night.

The next day he fished with the young men and they killed a seal. But the people did not draw him to them the way the Eiber villagers had. He saw no girl as pretty as Lito and none smiled upon him in the same way. So he became restless and at evening told the great hunter he must go on. The great one advised him to keep to the sea, being careful where he camped at night and wary of making any fire that could be seen from a distance. "The hill-devils will creep upon you at night and slay you," he said. "But the villages like this one will welcome you."

He slept that night with a strong wind blowing over him and the roaring of an angry sea lulling him into slumber. The next morning he prepared to leave. The women brought him a supply of fish and a cake of dried berries. The great hunter and many others launched their boats and went with him a mile or so. Metek was filled with wonder at the way the birchbark boat scudded along without the aid of a paddle. The villagers waved to him as he moved away from the shore and headed southward. Metek waved back; he would see these friendly people again when he returned.

Remembering the advice of the hunter, he kept well out beyond the booming surf which roared over the rocky coast line. On he pushed and did not go ashore until thirst forced him to seek the mouth of a river. Here he camped and slept without building a fire. He ate dried fish but threw away the fruit cake because he did not like the flavor of the rancid oil. Again he was alone, headed toward a country he had never seen but already he had tasted adventure and had seen new wonders. The villages ahead would hold much excitement for him and he would see many new things, like the ceremony he had just attended. He was eager to be on his way but he was tired from many hours of paddling and quickly fell asleep.

In the morning, he was glad he had hidden the kayak in a jumble of rocks and had slept well back from the beach in a clump of willow. The wet sand showed tracks of strange boots. Four men had passed that way moving up the river. The soles of their boots showed they were different from those of the hunters he had met. The leather was from a skin he had never seen. He looked about, but saw no one, and, after drinking and eating, launched his kayak and was off.

Stormy days came and the kayak was tossed and beaten by high seas. Fog and mist swirled about him and the air was raw and chill. When the sun finally broke through and the fog bank retreated, Metek saw before him what appeared to be an ocean river flowing steadily into the icy wastes he was leaving behind. He knew he had completed the circular course the great hunter had told him about and that this was the river which separated the two lands.

Metek let his kayak bob on the waves while he gazed out across Bering Strait toward the coast of Asia. Dimly the bold and lofty East Cape rose like a great sentinel, marking the Siberian mainland. It was thirty miles away, but as the fog disappeared it was clearly revealed. Turning back to his own shores, Metek stared at the abrupt walls of rock rising a thousand sheer feet from the sea, forming the rugged headland which was Cape Prince of Wales. From his northern approach this headland had seemed to slope gently upward, but now that he was swinging into the straits, it showed itself to be a mighty mountain of rock with towering faces.

The strong-flowing current began to sweep the kayak back along its course. Metek bent his back and began paddling. Ahead lay the two rocky islands the hunter had told him about, Noornabook and Ignalook. Midway, like stepping stones across the narrow waters, lay the barren islands. The largest looked about three miles long and a mile wide. Both rose steeply out of the sea to a height of seven or eight hundred feet. Metek fought to drive his light boat forward, and became so deeply engrossed in his fight that he had rounded the cape and was headed into a wide bay of placid waters before he saw the great village which lay on the sheltered shore.

His first knowledge of it came when he sighted the many boats with deerskin sails. They were much like the boat of the great hunter and some of them were sailing across the water while others lay on the beach. Beyond them he could see many people.

Metek slowed his pace and moved carefully. But soon he knew he would be welcome. The men in the sailing boats waved to him and shouted, while those on the shore gave him a friendly, welcome halloo. Metek put in and was soon surrounded by men, women, and children. The men helped him out of the kayak and carried it up to the village where they placed it on a rooftop to dry. They examined his implements and his weapons and they seemed to recognize the white man's knife he carried. Finally one hunter proudly displayed a knife which was almost the same. Metek was glad these people spoke his tongue well enough so that he could talk with them. They were Innuits, though their manner of life was so different and they had many words he did not know.

Their dress and their ways were much the same as in the other large village he had visited. He was fed and shown everything they owned, then the men sat with him and asked many questions. Again the hunters shook their heads when he said he was going south. There were many savage tribes, more, Metek gathered, to the south than any other place. Tribes lived deep in the hills and came down to the shore to kill and raid. Women were carried away and men were killed. These tribes did not live from the kill out of the sea but trapped and hunted inland. And they hated the Innuits. Metek must avoid them. But there were friendly sea-hunters who lived along the coast and upon the many islands he would come to. They did not speak the Innuit tongue but they were good people and great hunters. They were so great sea-hunters that they could kill the humpback whale. They would welcome Metek, but the others—the Chillkahts and the Awks and the Tahkoos—they would kill him if they met him.

Metek spent three days with the villagers. They supplied him with food and gave him a weapon which looked like a polished club, which they said would make killing Amikuk, the sea otter, very easy. He could walk up to the

curious beast and rap him over the head, that was all he
need do to get a meal of fresh meat.

When Metek left the village a dozen hunters in fast kayaks accompanied him until midday. They said good-by and
Metek began another circling course around Norton Sound
and down to the mouth of the great river every Innuit
hunter along the way had told him about.

He had passed along many miles of the Alaskan coast.
None of it had ever been mapped by white men, little of it
had ever been seen except by roving whalers or ships caught
in the ice pack and carried north by that monster to be
devoured by the ice itself. Those headlands, capes and bays
were without white-man's names and the Innuits had taken
the trouble to name only a few landmarks.

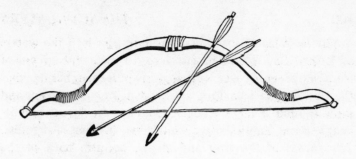

9. THE SEA-HUNTERS

One day Metek paddled across a wide belt of water flowing out to the sea and he knew that this was the mouth of a great river—the Yukon. The hundred mile delta of the Yukon is a blind labyrinth of misleading channels, sloughs and swamps. Metek passed country which was scarcely above the level of the tides; it seemed to him more like a vast inland sea filled with thousands of islets peeping above its surface, than the flat mouth of a river. Broader and narrower spaces between the low delta land showed and here its current was strongly marked by driftwood and logs plowing upon its muddy bosom as it wound through the marshes.

Metek shifted his course away from this dreary bog and kept clear of the muddy flood. No native ever penetrated the delta even though the air swarmed with myriads of breeding geese, ducks and wading birds, and the tall grass and sedge was alive with them. The curse of swarms of mosquitoes was more than even a stolid Innuit hunter could brave.

The trip around the delta was a long one and Metek was very weary when he swung in toward shore where cliffs and higher ground indicated the marsh had come to an end. He made camp on a bleak shore where he could find shelter in a rocky jumble of broken cliffs. To the west he could see an island looming out of the sea.

The next leg of his course brought him into the waters of Bristol Bay, where he cut across a turbulent stream of fresh water which was Nushugak river. Remembering what the hunter had told him, he headed into the stream and soon sighted a large village. This was Nushugak and its people were Innuits. Here Metek saw his first real forest. The shores of the river and all the country back of the village were thickly wooded with spruce forest, with groves of birch and poplar growing on the hillsides. Countless pools and lakes nestled in the hollows.

Again Metek was welcomed with food and many questions about his northern home. The people talked with a strange accent and many of their words were new to the boy. The younger men had their hair cut very short, some of their heads presenting shining spots that gleamed in the sunlight entirely without any covering of hair. The women and girls were red-lipped and smiling. Everyone welcomed Metek and talked to him.

In Nushugak the houses were different from any he had seen. Here the Innuits had plenty of wood and used it to build with. The houses were built with corner posts ten feet long set into the ground. Against these posts driftwood had been laid up for a wall. The chinking was of mud and sticks. Over this whole structure, sods of earth had been laid. A hole at the top let the light in. On rainy days this hole was covered by a thin sealskin that was almost transparent. Like the houses of his own people, the entrances here were underground passageways ten or twelve feet in length.

Most of the villagers were living in their summer homes and not in their houses. The summer huts were made with poles, upon which skins had been stretched. Bladders of oil and slabs of dried meat and fish hung above the reach of the dogs and the children. The vessels were of wood and there were a few stone pots. Metek missed nothing of the wonders about him. He meant to tell his people about them and to take a few things back as proof.

The Nushugak villagers were busy people. Many of them were far up the river hunting and fishing; others were inland taking birds and small fur-bearing animals. When Metek told them he was going south, they said he would come to the country of the sea-hunters who would welcome him. But they asked him to stay with them as they believed they had the finest hunting and fishing territory there was on earth. Metek agreed to stay a few days when they told him they were to have a night of entertainment very soon.

For two days he fished and hunted with the young men. In that time he proved he was their equal with a harpoon and a lance, even though he could not use the bow and arrow. In the surf he was a better boatman than any of them. On the evening of the ceremony Metek was very much excited. The ceremonies of these people seemed like wonders out of Kablunth's store of tales.

One of the young hunters took Metek to the meeting house, which was larger than any of the dwellings, and he seated himself among the men. On three sides of the room stone lamps had been lighted and the fire-hole had been covered with a skin. The guests began to sing to the sound of a drum, two men keeping them in order by beating time with sticks adorned with wolf's tails and gull's wings. The singing lasted a half hour. The songs praised the women who were to give the entertainment and promised them a reward of berries and deer-fat if they would show themselves.

When the song was finished the women appeared, and were received with much shouting and talking. The first to come brought a dish of food which she set before the men. They ate the food and praised the woman's cooking very loudly. Very soon a woman came who stood in the center of the hut and recited. As she recited she made motions to show how she gathered food, stored oil and did the daily work of a woman. When she told how she gathered berries and melted fat to make the delicious berry and oil mixture, the men bent forward eagerly. Then the woman brought a big bowl of the mixture and set it before the men. Her song grew faster and faster and the men leaned forward impatiently, their eyes on the food. Soon she passed wooden spoons among them and the song ended. There was no sound then except the munching of the men as they devoured the berries and oil. Metek ate his share and decided he liked these better than the first.

Other singers came and recited, telling how they prepared food. At the end of each song the women set the food before the men and they ate it. In this manner a very enjoyable evening passed and the men were well fed and sleepy when it was over. Metek and his friend went to bed and were soon asleep because such fine food was bound to bring sleep.

Metek would have stayed longer in the village, but he realized that the short summer was passing and he must hurry if he was to reach the southern villages where he would find white hunters. The Nushugak hunters said they had seen white-faced men. They were not sure these strangers lived to the south. Some of the men thought they lived in the middle of the great sea and came only as visitors. All agreed that Metek was foolish to seek them in their own villages. The white-faced ones were spirits, and could command magic. It was best to leave them alone.

From Nushugak, Metek headed south, but soon had to shift his course west because the coast line swerved. He had come to the great peninsula which marked the Aleutian chain, and he was traveling toward Asia. He noticed a change in the climate. The weather was stormy most of the time and there was much fog. He was worried by this change but kept paddling steadily. Black fogs swept in from the Bering Sea, blotting out everything. They were wet and chill and Metek was glad he was wearing his fur outfit. The sea life was different, too. He passed islands crowded with sea lions and several times a great rhytina rolled close to his kayak. The huge beast appeared to have no fear of the boat and stared at Metek out of mild eyes.

There were no villages on the rocky, storm-lashed coast, and few places where he could make a landing without braving ripping tides which raced between black rocks. Here he learned about Orca, the wolf of the sea. He was sliding along through a fast-sweeping fog when he came to a kelp bed where many sea lions played and sported. The lions had a shelter on a reef from which they moved out into the kelp beds to sport and fish. Metek was skirting the beds when he saw a lion playing in the open water beyond. As he looked, he saw five tall, black fins cutting the water close to the lion.

Metek watched the fast-moving fins as they swept toward the seal. He knew little about Orca, the killer, so he let his kayak glide and watched. A native hunter of that region would have headed for shore at once, for Orca attacks anything he comes upon, even the great whales. He saw the killers roll up out of the sea and spew oily water into the air. The lion saw them, too, and streaked for the kelp bed in a frantic dash.

The pack cut after him with terrific speed. They closed upon him and their long, slashing teeth ripped him into shreds. The water boiled red as they made their kill. In a few minutes they had devoured the luckless lion and turned toward the kelp beds. Like wolves, they hunted in a pack, dividing the kill in savage haste, slaughtering anything they came upon. Metek suddenly realized that here was a beast that would attack man. He shot the kayak toward the kelp beds and when it swerved the killers sighted it. The black fins cut the water as the five fifteen-foot monsters charged upon Metek. Driving his paddle deep, he headed for shore.

The killers were close upon him when he beached the kayak, taking advantage of a great wave to dart high up on a narrow strip of sand. The leader of the pack was so close to the stern of the boat that he did not turn back and Metek found himself and the whale high and dry on land.

The killer lashed and floundered in an attempt to get back to the sea but the wave had been a very big one and none so large came again. Metek freed himself from the kayak and stood watching while the whale flopped and rolled until he brought himself up against a ledge of rocks. Metek sat down to wait until the big one became weak. He waited for a half hour, then attacked the whale, driving his lance into him many times.

Here was a great feast of highly-prized meat, enough for a whole village. Metek wished he had friends to join him. He set about cutting away large pieces of the rich blubber. He ate a tremendous amount but what he took did not diminish the supply. That night he slept close to his kill and the next day he feasted again. He would have stayed longer but the fog and a cold rain came and he decided to move on until he came to the villages of the sea-hunters.

Now he was careful to keep a sharp watch for packs of killer whales. He saw several but they were far away and did not molest him. At last he came to a broad channel of water which cut through the rocky backbone of the peninsula. He turned south, heading through the channel, and within half a day had passed out of the Bering Sea and into the Pacific. And now he knew he had been following a narrow strip of land which thrust itself out into the ocean.

He headed east again along the southern shore of the peninsula.

This coast was more sheltered from the wind, but the tides ran like mill races and the sea was terrible in its wild lashing. The mists and the chill remained, but now there was more rain than before. One day Metek entered a wide bay, hoping to make a landing where he could build a driftwood fire and dry his clothing. He was delayed by a drama of the sea which held him in awe as he watched.

A great humpback whale was rolling and diving, lunging and cutting in great circles. The water which foamed in his wake was bloody. Around him, darting in, lashing at him, was a pack of killer whales. The monster was bigger a hundred times than his assailants, but he could not strike them with his tail or smash them with his body. They circled and attacked and circled, ripping the great mouth of the humpback until he dived deep.

When the mammoth dived the killers circled about savagely, leaping out of the water so that their black bodies gleamed in the dull light. They paid no attention to Metek's boat, if they saw it. Then the humpback came up and they attacked him again. He fought savagely, whipping the sea to boiling foam, then he went down again, but this time his wounds kept him from staying under overlong. Metek would have stayed to watch the finish, which he knew was sure to come, but fog rolled in and enveloped the bay, closing around him in a dense wall. Through the mist he could see the bulk of the whale rolling helplessly on the surface with the killers slashing him, feeding savagely. Orca, the gladiator, was a terrible one. Metek made off through the mist in search of a beach where he could land.

He found no beach for several miles and when he did locate a harbor he saw huts back from the shore and strange boats pulled up on the beach. A number of men stood beside the boats. Silently they watched as Metek paddled toward them. They were not Innuits; Metek was certain of that. He had never seen natives like them before. But when he lifted his hand in welcome they answered him and came down to the shore as he beached his kayak.

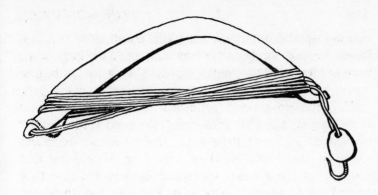

10. THE WHITE MEN

Metek soon discovered that he was barely able to make himself understood by his new friends. Their talk was as different from his as were their ways and their boats. But Metek understood that they were having great trouble. They tried to make him understand that he should get into his kayak and leave. When he failed to understand they shrugged their shoulders and led him up the hill to their village.

The Aleut men were short, with broad faces and high cheekbones. Their hair was long and black, while the eyes had a trace of Mongolian slant. Metek went with them, wondering what was troubling them. Their welcome to him had been extended readily, so that he was sure it was not because of his coming. He tried to ask about white men but could not make them understand.

The village was a cluster of sod and driftwood huts. Everyone was in a state of excitement. Some of the families were packing their things together and piling them outside the huts. The others sat and watched, shaking their heads and arguing. Metek wondered why part of the villagers should be deserting their homes in such a hurry. He did not have long to wait for an explanation. A man came

107

running up the beach shouting and pointing to the bay. Metek looked, as did all of the villagers. Two large boats were headed in to the landing beach. They were the biggest Metek had ever seen and they were driven by many oars.

The villagers seemed paralyzed with fear. Those who were holding things in their hands dropped them. Several women ducked into their huts. The others all stood and stared at the boats. As they drew near, Metek saw that the men in them were white-faced hunters and that they carried magic weapons such as he had seen the white men use. But it was clear that the sea-hunters feared these men. Most of them had been trying to get their things together and run away. They seemed to have been expecting the white men.

The two whaleboats beached and the sailors got out of them. A tall man snapped orders and the sailors shouldered their guns and began marching up to the villagers. The Aleuts did not move or say anything; they just stood staring at the Russian and his Cossacks. Metek watched eagerly. He had no fear of the white men, but he did not move to greet them.

Kosiloff halted his men before the villagers. He was a Russian adventurer and explorer and his discovery of the bleak and stormy Aleutian coast had been a very fortunate one for him. Here he had found the island, the reefs and the kelp beds swarming with sea otter. The pelt of the sea otter was worth more than a hundred skins of any other animal. In the China markets, this robe of kings brought fabulous prices. And Kosiloff had found slaves who could be forced to hunt the otter. The Aleuts were expert otter hunters and knew how to catch the cunning beasts.

Kosiloff's crew was composed of Cossacks, rough-look-ing fellows of small size, lean and wiry, with large, thin-lipped mouths and skins leathery from the wind and salt spray. They were the offspring of Creole Russian Tartars and women from the native tribes of Siberia. They were a dirty and a cruel lot, placing no restraint upon their actions when facing the peace-loving Aleuts. Kosiloff snapped an order and one of the men, who looked more like a native than the others, stepped forward.

The Cossack sailor began talking rapidly, waving his arms and pointing to the row of boats on the beach. He told the Aleuts that Kosiloff wanted ten boats and twenty hunters. The Aleuts stared at the Russian sullenly. They had heard about the Russians from their neighbors who lived beyond the point. Kosiloff made the hunters take sea otters for him. He drove the natives and fed them poorly, and he paid no wages for the work. If an Aleut tried to escape he was shot down.

Metek watched and listened, able to understand only a few words, but able to feel the fear that had taken hold of the sea-hunters. Kosiloff paced back and forth pointing to the men he wanted. He picked the strongest and youngest men. Suddenly he halted before Metek and sized up the stocky Innuit.

"Take this one," he said in Russian.

One of the sailors shoved Metek over beside an Aleutian hunter. Metek stood still, only vaguely understanding what was going on. An old man stepped forward and began talking to the Cossack interpreter. He waved his hands and spoke rapidly.

If the hunters were taken away there would be no one to get food for the women and children, the old man explained. The interpreter repeated the message to Kosiloff. With a frown the Russian advanced upon the old man. He whipped out his sword and struck the old fellow with the flat side of the blade, knocking him down.

No one else argued with the Russian after that. The Aleuts went quietly down to the beach and Metek went with them. As they got into their bidarkas, two men to each boat, the interpreter explained that if any of the boatmen tried to run away the Cossacks would open fire from the whaleboats. The Aleuts knew the terrible power of the white-men's weapons. They nodded their heads and shrugged their shoulders, resigning themselves to their fate. They had been told that if a Cossack fired a rifle ball at them the ball would follow them until it overtook and killed its victim. They believed this to be true because they had had very little contact with guns.

Metek got into one of the bidarkas and the Aleut who was to be his partner put him in front where the lanceman and harpooner sat. The bidarkas were shoved off and they waited for the big boats to row away from the shore. The bidarkas were built much as Metek's kayak was constructed. The frame was slender and light with a covering of untanned lionskin stretched over it. The skin covering had been sewed on green and had dried as taut as a drumhead. It was smeared with thick seal oil, which kept the water from soaking through it for from twenty-four to thirty-six hours. A soaked bidarka had to be hauled out and dried. Kosiloff had discovered this and had decided he needed an extra crew and set of boats so he could have a group constantly hunting. While one group was drying their boats the other could be working.

The bidarkas danced along ahead of the heavy boats. The Aleuts made no attempt to move off though they could easily have slipped away from the clumsy rowboats. Across the bay they went and on around a high cliff to another cove where Metek saw his first sailing vessel. The *Petr* lay alongside a great rock, made fast fore and aft. Her canvas was snug and her spars stood out against the

gray sky. Metek stared at her in wonder. He suddenly
realized that there had been just such a boat down under
the ice back in the cove on the island where he had found
the first traces of white men.

As sailing vessels go, the *Petr* was a sorry ship. She was
Russian, built with Cossack labor. Her timbers had been
hewn from green logs with axes and lashed together with
leather thongs because there were no iron spikes or nails in
Petropavlovsk on the Kamchatka coast. Her sailcloth was
ragged and her hawsers had been spliced in many places
because they had been cut into lengths which could be
packed on shaggy ponies and carried across the wastes of
Inner Siberia. No people ever braved storm-ridden seas in
such boats. The Cossack crews were not trained to the sea
and knew nothing better in the way of ships and the mas-
ters who sailed the crazy ships were reckless and daring,
willing to risk anything to get across to the islands and
bays where the otters were found.

But to Metek the *Petr* was a magnificent kayak, a thing
of awesome size, so great that it must be master of the sea.
He could not conceal his curiosity and bent forward eagerly as they drew near the side of the vessel. He tried to talk
to his companion but the Aleut refused to answer. He was
staring up at the deck of the ship grimly.

On the shore near the great rock was a camp of Aleuts.
Their bidarkas lay on the shore drying. They did not greet
the newcomers, but remained seated watching them. They
were gaunt-faced, hungry-looking fellows. Five sailors with
rifles stood guard over the camp. The newcomers unloaded
and pulled their bidarkas out on the rocks. They walked
over to the little fires around which the others were huddled. In a few minutes low-voiced talk broke out.

Metek stood watching the scene. He started to join his
companion when the interpreter spoke to him sharply.

Metek was startled. The man was speaking in the Innuit tongue.

"Where did you come from?" he asked.

"From far to the north. I came seeking the white hunters," Metek said.

The man laughed. "You will not be glad you found them," he said.

"How do you speak my tongue?" Metek asked.

"I lived five years among the people to the north. Our ship was wrecked and they took me in." The man scowled. "I should have stayed with them. This Russian is a money-mad fool. All he thinks of is more otter and then more otter. The natives will rise up and massacre all of us." He stared at Metek and added savagely, "But if you say a word of this to anyone you will be killed."

"I can talk to no one," Metek said. "I came to get one of the magic weapons to take to my people so they can kill game as the white hunters do."

"Kosiloff will never let any native get away with a gun," the interpreter said, and smiled sourly. "I, Ivan, know that, for I tried to run away with one."

Metek did not know whether to consider Ivan as a friend or not. He was beginning to fear his captors, and yet he had a great curiosity about them. Ivan had a scar across his cheek and neck, a scar that was livid and not long healed. Metek guessed correctly that the man had been caught trying to steal a gun. But he meant to ask for one, to offer in trade his lance and harpoon. He would not steal one.

"I would give my lance and harpoon in trade for the gun," he said.

Ivan laughed harshly. "Kosiloff will take what he wants from you and give you nothing but dog meat and little enough of that. You'll work every day as long as there is any light." Ivan lifted a hand and his fingers touched the scar on his neck. "But I will do what I can for you. Your people saved me from freezing and starving. They are decent people and not like this Russian. Do not expect much, for I am little better off than those slaves." He turned and strode toward the ship.

Metek sat down with the Aleuts. They had a little meat of very poor quality. It was old and dry but they were heating it over the fires and eating it. It seemed odd that men should be starving with the sea and the air teeming with food. But Kosiloff allowed none of the men to take time for hunting food. He meant to fill his hold with otter pelts and get away from the reefs before the fall storms struck. Kalan—that was his watchword—kalan, the fabulous pelt that brought much gold.

Metek was not hungry enough to eat any of the meat. He sat looking at the great ship, wondering what the deck was like and what was in the space below it. He could see Cossacks moving about on board. They went armed as though afraid of an attack. Then he watched the guards standing about and saw that they, too, were always alert, their guns kept close to their hands. These hard men could not understand the passive way the Aleuts submitted to harsh treatment. It seemed to them that the natives must sooner or later revolt.

11. AMIKUK

Before the coming of the Russians, Amikuk, the sea otter, lived a happy life. He had enemies: Orca, the killer whale, the Aleuts, who occasionally went otter hunting, and a few lesser hunters. But his sharp wits and his flashing speed in the surf kept him safe so that his tribe prospered and grew.

Where the roaring breakers foamed over ragged reefs and the rip tides raced with boiling fury, under skies which seldom cleared of damp fog, Amikuk and his fellows played and hunted and slept. The kelp beds offered shelter from Orca and the deep marine ridges offered food. Life on the reef was wild and free. Upon the kelp beds and the rocky shore the sea otters basked in the brief hours of sunshine. Those on the shore curled up like dogs, their black and brown robes gleaming in the sunlight. Those basking on the kelp beds always dozed on their broad backs, their forearms clasped over their breasts, their big, brown eyes staring up into the sky.

The baby otters lay on their mothers' breasts, held there snugly, nestled in a soft bed of fur. After each nap the little ones would stir and lift their heads. Then the mother otter would move lazily, lifting her baby above her face, making gentle noises in her throat. After that she would playfully toss the little one into the water. Squealing and kicking, the youngster would go down until the green water

116

filled its mouth. Down, down, its little body twisting, its legs working frantically, while a string of silver bubbles spiraled upward. Then the mother would roll over and dive after her young, bringing it to the surface where she would toss it into the air. Little Amikuk would curl up into a ball of fur. Then the mother would pull the babe to her, hugging and kissing it as a human mother would. Time after time she would toss her baby into the water and repeat the same performance. This was her way of training the little one to swim. She was careful not to let it sink too deep or become too much afraid.

After a half hour of play the little one would become weary and say very plainly that it did not want to play any more. Then the mother would shake the water from its coat and wash its face. After this was done she would carefully lay the baby on a broad mass of kelp where it would lie staring up into the sky, keeping very still while she dived for food. With a powerful thrust of her lithe body she would dive, straight down, a stream of silver bubbles twisting up behind her.

Swiftly she would slide down into the twilight of the sea. At a hundred feet down she would locate a ridge where sea life swarmed. Her paws would swiftly locate a fat sea urchin, then she would curve upward. No other animal save the seal could make such a dive, or return so swiftly. Breaking water beside the kelp cradle where the young one lay, she would turn upon her back. Placing the sea urchin upon her breast, she would tear it in halves, eating the contents of each half, then tossing the shell far out across the water. With great care she would wash her face and hands, then dive again.

Out beyond the kelp beds, where the wind lashed the sea into rolling lanes of white-capped waves, the male otters would be playing, diving through the air or deep

down into the sea, jumping, plunging, with backs arched or
bellies up. Their backs always went up like the beaver's
when they dived; their bellies were always up when they
drove ahead. On calm days they did not play. It was only
when the surf roared and lashed the reef, and the breakers
ran high, when the winds and the waves challenged their
strength that they sported.

Their favorite game was tag, a sort of follow-the-leader
game. One swift male would lead the chase, making a wide
circle. His back would go up as he dived, down, down,
bubbles dancing behind him. He knew exactly where the
deep-down ridges lay. Settling upon the ridge, he would
search about in the dim light. He was unhurried because
he could stay down for ten minutes if need be. Locating
a fat squid he would jerk it free with a swift movement,
then rise to the surface. Floating on his back, he would
dine with his dinner spread upon the broad, flat table of
his breast. His fellows would follow his example and a
great feast would be made.

Amikuk was four feet in length, with fur of brownish
black. Wrapped about him was a robe more highly prized
by hunters than any other, the robe of kings and princes,
priceless in the market places of the world. The prized
possession did not worry the otter. It served him well in
keeping out the cold water and the chill wind, but he did
not consider it beyond that. Nor did the native hunters
prize his robe greatly. They liked better the pelt of the
fur-seal and the flesh of the sea lion.

After the feast the males played their game again. They
went sailing, shooting, diving with their backs to the deep,
their shining breasts to the sky. With the speed and ease of
a porpoise at sea they broke through the billows, leaping
across the trough to dart into the green wall beyond, each
otter chasing the one ahead. Their course was a twisting,

circling one, like the trail of a sea serpent. Tiring of the game, they would return to the kelp bed or to the rocky shore where they would crowd together and lie down to sleep. On land they were clumsy and slow of movement, unlike their brother, the land otter. They were children of the sea and the storm, but they liked to gather in a rocky cove where the sun beat upon the rocks.

Into this paradise came Kosiloff and his Cossacks. They saw the hordes of kalans and were amazed. Never had they seen the sea otter in such great numbers, and never so tame and easily approached. Wild with a lust to kill and secure the valuable skins, they landed upon the beaches with clubs and guns and slaughtered every otter they could. They did not spare the mothers with babes, nor the half-grown animals. The shore ran red with the blood of their victims.

But very soon the otters left the beaches and sought refuge on the reefs and out in the sea. Soon they were to become sea animals, never landing upon the shore except when sick or injured. This made the Russians seek new ways to slaughter the kalan and brought about the Aleutian slavery.

Metek's arrival came at a time when Kosiloff was developing his system. He was greedy to skim the cream from this locality before a swarm of Russian boats came to the hunting grounds. Every big catch that was taken back to Siberia caused a dozen new expeditions to start out. Never had the miserably poor Cossack hunters had such an opportunity to secure wealth.

The morning after his capture, Metek took his place in a bidarka. He soon demonstrated that he was an expert paddler, so he wielded the paddle while his Aleutian companion sat ahead and manned the weapons of the kill. With a Cossack crew of riflemen following them the Aleuts set out for a reef where they would hunt. Amikuk had taken flight to a habitat which would give him protection. The reef was gloomy, beaten by wind and waves, lashed by sleet and rain and persistent fog. It extended far out from the protecting cliffs along the shore. There hurricane gales swept down out of the northern wastes and the currents raced in and out of the passages between the black rocks.

The Cossack boatmen stayed clear of the turbulent grounds, depending upon their rifles, and the fear of the Aleuts, to make sure the hunters did not steal off into the fog, and that they hunted with all of their skill.

The first hunt Metek joined was a surround, made possible by the weather, which had been calmer than usual for two days, and the sea which was not running with its usual fury. The bidarkas spread out in a long line, keeping well abreast, with an interval of a hundred feet between boats. In this way the hunters paddled swiftly and silently over the water, each man peering sharply into the tumbling water ahead, watching for the blunt nose of Amikuk, should he poke it above the surface of the sea to catch his breath.

Suddenly an otter was discovered, apparently sleeping near a mass of kelp. The discoverer made a quiet signal which was flashed along the line. Not a word was spoken, not a paddle splashed, but the sensitive Amikuk took alarm, and with powerful strokes of his webbed feet, shot down into the depths and sped away. The Aleutian boatman nearest the spot where the otter dived sent his bidarka to the spot and hoisted his paddle. Instantly the other boats darted off, forming a great circle around the Aleut with the upraised paddle.

Amikuk would have to rise to the surface somewhere within sight of the sharp eyes of the hunters. Ten minutes passed, then a hunter shouted and hurled his harpoon.

He had sighted the otter's nose as it broke water. The hunter's paddle-man sent the bidarka darting toward the spot, where he took up a position with his paddle upraised. Again the circle formed and the hunters waited.

Time after time Amikuk came up to snatch a breath of air. Never was he given space to fill his lungs, but was allowed only a gasp of air before he had to dive to dodge the harpoons and spears hurled at him. The hunter in Metek's craft had scored a hit upon the weary otter which brought a gush of blood to the water. Under the ancient rules of the chase, the otter, when captured, would belong to this man. Under the rules of Kosiloff the pelt would be taken over by the Cossacks.

At last the luckless Amikuk became so filled with gases and so tired from his exertions and the lack of air that he could no longer dive. The hunters swarmed around and dispatched him. Then the *Petr's* tender boat rowed up and took the otter. The Cossacks would strip off the pelt while the Aleuts located another victim.

All day the hunters worked, killing many otters. When dusk began to settle and heavy fog rolled in from the sea the weary band turned back to their miserable camp. Metek's body ached; he was wet and cold and hungry. That night he ate the stringy meat the Cossacks tossed to him and later huddled close to a fire so that his clothes would dry.

The next morning the sea was rough and ugly. It came rolling in under the lashing of a gale which drove sleet and rain before it. The waves came in threes with the third and largest smashing against the *Petr* and foaming over her deck. Since there was no surround possible, Kosiloff ordered a surf hunt. Metek had never hunted in that fashion and the Cossacks shouted at him and kicked him because he did not know how.

The surf hunt was the most exciting and venturesome of all the hunts engaged in by the Aleuts. When the hunters reached the shelter of a high bluff, they crouched there peering out at the foaming, swiftly running water. Out on the point the wind blew so hard a man could not stand against its fury. It shrieked in a weird crescendo as it literally ripped the crests of the breakers into tatters.

Four of the Aleuts made ready for the dangerous trial. No amount of shouting or threatening by the Cossacks was of any avail. Only two bidarkas would go. The Aleuts maintained that only four men need risk the fury of the storm. They got into their bidarkas in the lee of the bluff and lashed their jackets water-tight around the rims of the manholes. In a moment the four struck out beyond the protection of the cliff into the very vortex of the sea, and scudding like an arrow before the wind they disappeared into the storm.

To the Russians this seemed like suicide and they did not try to follow, but the Aleuts knew that within two hours the blow would slacken and that within that time they could reach a sheltered inlet where a series of little islands and rocks lay awash. The men drove their frail boats down wind, battling with their paddles.

They reached the sheltered inlet and as they had guessed the storm began to subside. Here some fifty sea otters had taken refuge from the open sea. They lay with their heads buried under heaps of seaweed to avoid the pelting of the wind, sleeping out the storm. The four Aleuts crept up on the sleeping otters. They carried blunt wooden clubs in their hands and they made no attempt to move quietly as the noise of the surf drowned every sound they made. Swiftly the Aleuts dealt death to the sleeping otters, whacking them over the head with their clubs and flinging their bodies free of the kelp. In less than an hour the four hunters had slain more than forty of the animals.

Greedy for spoils, the Cossacks, led by Kosiloff, followed as soon as the wind died down. Their greed was greater than their fear of the high seas and when they saw the number of otters the hunters had taken they set up a wild shout and fell upon the carcasses with their sharp knives. Kosiloff was so well pleased that he gave a present of tobacco to each of the four hunters.

That night while the sea-hunters sat huddled around their driftwood fires the storm returned with greater fury than before and the sleet turned to snow. The Aleuts knew this was a danger signal warning them that the brief summer was waning and that winter's ice and snow might come to stay. The Cossacks were frightened, but Kosiloff laughed at them, reminding them that they, that day, had taken forty kalans worth five hundred silver rubles each. He asked them if they intended letting a blow drive them away from such wealth.

The Cossacks shrugged their shoulders and scowled at the skipper of the *Petr*. They were greedy and wanted all the silver they could get their hands on but they had a great fear of the northern seas when they began foaming and rolling under driving snow. They finally agreed to stay and hunt.

The elements forced a change in Kosiloff's plans that night. As the waves mounted, they threatened to lift the *Petr* and toss her bodily over the rock to which she was lashed. Kosiloff set his men to working ship in a desperate attempt to escape out to sea. Every sailor was needed on deck so that he was forced to call even the guards from the Aleut camp. Ivan told the sea-hunters that they might return to their village.

The Aleuts sat huddled in their fur robes and watched the big ship fight her way clear of the rock. She wallowed and plunged but finally put out to sea and vanished into the swirling wall of snow. The Aleuts did not try to face the storm but remained in camp through the night.

The next morning found the storm still beating but with lessened fury. The Aleuts stirred themselves and made ready to challenge the angry sea. They launched their cockleshell boats and slid out into the seething water. Metek took his place in the bidarka he had been helping to paddle. The sea-hunters now considered him one of their people.

With skill as great as that of the otter or the seal, the Aleuts skirted the black rocks along the promontory and headed into the calmer waters of their own bay. They were eager to return home to the warmth and the good food they would find in their huts. The whole village was down on the beach as soon as the hunters were sighted, and the welcome was a warm one. Great excitement prevailed, not only because of the return of the hunters whom the villagers had given up as dead, but because a school of humpback whales had been sighted.

Among the Aleuts, the appearance of Ahgashitnak, the yearling whale, and Akhoak, the calf whale, was a great event, and even the terrible experience with the Cossacks could not keep them from making a great hunt. Metek, who now understood much that was said, was as excited as any of the others.

There was much rejoicing, too, because the returning hunters reported that the great spirit of the sea had become so angry over the wanton slaughter of her children, the otters, that she had swallowed up the white-man's ship.

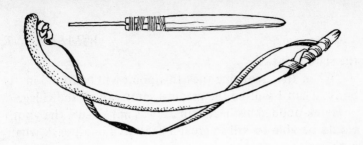

12. WHALE HUNT

No food was so highly prized by the Aleuts as the blubber and gristle of a whale. To secure this prize, the sea-hunters undertook great dangers and hardships. Many times they were bitterly disappointed, but they always tried.

Metek watched and listened and what he saw and heard made him admire the Aleut hunters more than ever. The humpback whale is a lean, fighting monster, which, when harpooned, dives and runs like an express train for fifty miles or more taking with it a boat and its crew, if that boat cannot free itself. The Cossack whalers avoided the humpback because he was unmanageable and savage.

From a lookout on the shore, Metek watched the school of whales in the bay. Under the lee of the north shore the school played and fed, rising and sinking, their broad, gray-black backs gleaming wetly. They went down lazily, rising again with a sonorous whistle as they "blew". A cloud of whale-birds hovered over the area occupied by the monsters and finally settled upon the water to share the feast of the big ones.

One of the young men showed Metek how he was preparing to kill Ahgashitnak. His sole weapon was a spear handle of wood about six feet long; to the head of this he lashed a smoothly polished socket of walrus ivory, in which he inserted a tip of serrated slate that resembled a huge arrowhead, twelve inches long and four broad at the barbs. He grinned up at Metek as he carved his mark deeply upon

125

the slate point.

"When the great one dies this point will be found in his body. Then I will be the greatest hunter of all the village."

Metek nodded his head, but he was not so sure the youth would be able to kill so great a beast as a humpback whale with such a weapon.

When the weapon was ready, the young hunter told Metek he might have the honor of paddling the bidarka for him. Metek was eager for the sport. They joined the other hunters on the beach and made ready to try for a kill. The boats slid out into the sheltered cove and darted away toward the school of feeding whales. The great, fish-like beasts paid no attention to the bidarkas as the boats approached. Up and down they rolled, boiling the sea, whistling as they rose. Metek's friend motioned toward a yearling whale a few yards away. He was avoiding an old bull or a grown cow. Metek shot the bidarka in close. The whale seemed as big as the white-man's ship as they slid in beside it.

The whale sank down and Metek held the boat. Up came the yearling rounding his glistening back out of the water close to the bidarka. The young Aleut raised his weapon and signaled for Metek to be ready for an instant retreat. The spear flashed across the water, driven by all the force the hunter could put behind it. The barb struck the whale just under the stubby dorsal fin. The wooden shaft was at once detached as the whale sprang into action. With a great splash the marine monster went down, his contortions driving the spearhead deeper and deeper into his body. Metek was called upon for all his skill in order to pull the bidarka clear of the lashing flukes of the beast.

When they were clear of the swirling water where the whale had dived the Aleut nodded toward the shore. Metek saw that all of the other hunters were returning to the beach. He was disappointed for he had thought they were to fight a savage battle with one of the whales. When they had landed Metek's friend explained the hunt to him.

The wounded whales would make for the open sea where they would "go to sleep" for three days, then death would come and gases of decomposition would cause the monster to float. If the spirit of the sea was kind the currents and the winds would beach the whale somewhere near the village. For the next week it would be the duty of every man, woman and child to climb to a high point from which he could watch for the prize.

The lucky hunter whose spearhead killed the whale would be much honored and if during his life he made a score of three or more whales his body, when he died, would be divided into small pieces and kept by his living relatives and friends to rub upon their spear points. Metek's friend proudly showed him such a lucky bit which he had received the winter before. The luck charm was from a hunter who had killed seven whales in his long life. The young Aleut was certain so potent a charm could not fail to bring him great honor.

Waiting for the whale to end his long sleep was a busy three days. Every villager spent all of his time on the cliffs watching the sea. The fourth day came, and the fifth. Disappointment began to show on the faces of the hunters. Perhaps the great spirit of the sea was displeased and would not send them a prize. Metek shared their worry as well as their long vigils.

On the sixth day a hunter came leaping down from a cliff shouting, "Ahgashitnak! Ahgashitnak!" He pointed to the south as he ran.

The villagers swarmed to the cliff from which the hunter had descended. Metek raced beside his friend, Kagia. Kagia was shouting like a wild man. He was sure the whale was his kill. Eagerly every eye peered out to sea. The hunter was right, a strong current and a steady wind was bringing the carcass of a whale to the beach below. The great body bobbed and rolled as it moved shoreward.

With wild shouts, the villagers raced back to their huts to secure knives and pots, then they streamed down to the beach where they waded out into the icy water, waving their knives and dancing up and down.

"See! See! The big one is Ahgashitnak, the yearling!" Kagia shouted as he pounded Metek across the back.

Slowly the massive mountain of flesh moved in until it was awash upon the beach. In a few moments the Aleuts were swarming around it, unmindful of the soaking they got from the incoming waves. Great chunks of blubber and gristle were cut away and carried to the beach. Fires were built and a feast began. Later much meat would be hauled to the village, but at the moment there was no thought of going farther than beyond the reach of the waves.

Kagia, between mouthfuls of luscious blubber, explained sadly that he was afraid the village would be without honor because the whale was so big they would not be able to devour it in one day. Among the Aleuts a village was great and powerful if its people could make away with the flesh of a whale within a single day. Metek looked at the whale and agreed with Kagia. If that monster had to be eaten within twenty-four hours in order to save the honor of the village, then he feared the people would be without honor.

After stuffing themselves for five hours the sea-hunters set about cutting into the carcass to recover the spear point. There was much excitement as the older men slashed through gristle and blubber, following the path of the shaft. At length they uncovered it and carried it to the fires where it was cleaned and examined for the mark of its owner.

Kagia and Metek crowded close. Metek had a stake in the honor should the point carry Kagia's mark because he had paddled for the young hunter.

"It is mine," shouted a lean-faced Aleut, as he reached for the point.

Kagia stepped back, then leaped forward. "No! It is mine!" he shouted.

The two hunters bent over the point. Kagia's mark was the eye of a gull with a feather above it. The older hunter slowly passed the spearhead to the boy.

"It is yours," he said.

Everyone crowded around Metek and Kagia shouting and slapping them across the shoulders. Metek received very nearly as much attention as Kagia. The two were seated upon the sand and the women brought choice morsels of gristle, done brown over the coals. The men brought the fattest strips of blubber and presented them. Metek and Kagia had already eaten an unbelievable amount of meat, but they accepted the delicacies and munched them happily.

The ceremony was interrupted by a shout from one of the men. He was pointing to the bay. All eyes turned that way and silence settled upon the merrymakers. Out of a black bank of fog slid the *Petr,* her canvas bellying as she plowed toward the beach.

The Aleuts were stunned by the coming of the Russian ship they had thought destroyed by the storm. Their faces, which had been smiling and happy a few minutes before, became expressionless. The gay feast had suddenly become a grim gathering. Slowly the men turned and marched up the beach toward the village. The return of Kosiloff could mean nothing but disaster to many of them.

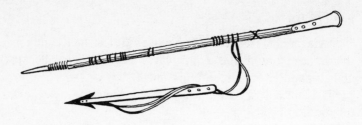

13. THE WHITE-MAN'S SHIP

The *Petr* slid into calm water under the lee of the cliffs and dropped her anchor. She lay against the gray cliffs like a wounded gull, her canvas ripped and torn, her foremast twisted. Standing before their village, the Aleuts watched the ship. No boats came ashore and after two hours of waiting the sea-hunters began stirring about. A number of the women returned to the carcass of the whale and began cutting slabs of blubber and gristle which they carried up to the village.

On board the *Petr*, Kosiloff was bellowing and driving his weary Cossacks. The men had labored without rest for several days in order to save the ship. Now that they had reached the haven of a snug harbor they wanted to rest. Kosiloff wanted to get the ship repaired so that he could push on to new hunting grounds. He planned to take a great many more kalans before turning across the north Pacific. The crew was ready to head home at once. In surly silence, they set to work repairing the mast and the canvas.

Ivan had been moving about among the men and Kosiloff kept a close watch upon him. He suspected Ivan of telling the crew they should not stay but must insist upon leaving the stormy coast as soon as possible. At last he called Ivan to him. The Cossack moved across the deck and stood before the ship's master.

"You would go home?" Kosiloff asked.

"Winter is coming and with it the ice," Ivan said. "We

130

have a fortune in the hold and each has a share in it."

"But I am master of the *Petr,* is that right?" Kosiloff's bearded face was expressionless but his eyes were hard and cold.

"You are the master and will do as you wish," Ivan agreed.

"I will do as I wish," Kosiloff said very softly. "And if any man talks mutiny I will hang him from a yardarm."

Ivan nodded. He knew the master would do just that. Kosiloff would not hesitate to hang a man for much less than mutiny. He waited for Kosiloff to go on. The master smiled and his red beard parted. He removed his greasy cap and ran his thick fingers through his shock of flaming hair. Kosiloff was a huge man, short but broad across the shoulders, with massive legs that bulged tightly inside his leather breeches.

"I should not enjoy hanging you, Ivan," he said. "You are as near to a mate as I have."

Ivan smiled, a thin-lipped smile, and his eyes met Kosiloff's cold, blue stare. He said nothing.

"Now go and see that the men make repairs quickly. While we lie here idle I would have you take on a store of meat." The master turned away as he finished speaking.

Ivan went back to his work. He knew that there wasn't a Cossack in the crew who would hesitate to go to Kosiloff and tell him anything his mate said that might hint at mutiny. Even though the men wanted to go back to their home port, yet they would curry favor with the master, because they naturally disliked anyone in authority, and Ivan had been the one who gave Kosiloff's orders when those orders were disagreeable. He drove the men to their work, threatening the obstinate members with a heavy spike. The Cossacks understood this type of leadership, and worked.

For two days the crew worked repairing the damage done by the storm. When they had finished, the *Petr* looked a bit less ragged and ill-fitted. Her canvas was tight and her mast was straight, but Ivan's trained eye saw that the repairs had been crudely made and would not stand another bad storm. His face was glum as he went forward to report to Kosiloff. He found the master leaning over the rail staring across the bay toward the Aleutian village.

"The repairs are made, sir," he said.

Kosiloff turned about. "Secure a supply of food," he said, and returned to his speculations.

"I will take a party and kill sea cow," Ivan replied.

Kosiloff did not answer. He was busy with thoughts of future hunting trips. He wanted to locate new otter grounds where the animals could be taken on the shore. He believed that across the peninsula to the north he would find such grounds, islands and reefs where Amikuk had not learned to fear the white hunters.

Ivan ordered eight men into a boat which had been lowered. He had sighted a sea cow in the bay and knew the beast offered easy prey and excellent meat which could be salted and stored in casks like pork.

The rhytina was a curious beast, the largest of all the Sirenia, growing to a length of thirty feet. Its large size and its slowness, along with its utter fearlessness of man, made it the easiest creature in the north to kill, and marked it for quick extinction. It was plentiful in the bay and Ivan soon located one swimming slowly along, its great, blunt head rippling the water. He ordered the men to put in close to the beast.

The Cossacks slid the boat alongside the sea cow. Ivan sat in the bow with a musket across his knees. The rhytina paid no attention to the boat, except to change its course enough to swim past the craft. It regarded Ivan with expressionless eyes which showed no trace of fear or curiosity. Ivan took aim with his gun muzzle less than a yard from the sea cow. His gun roared and belched black powder smoke. The rhytina shuddered and writhed. Instantly one of the Cossacks drove a heavy harpoon into the beast and the others began rowing toward the *Petr*.

Loading the rhytina onto the ship and cutting it up was the work of all hands. Casks were brought on deck and the meat was sliced and salted, then packed into the casks. By the end of the day a full supply of salt meat was packed below decks. Ivan had lived among the Innuits long enough to have acquired a taste for raw blubber. He sat on a cask cutting strips of fresh meat and eating them. The Cossack sailors watched him for a time and finally joined him. They were all seated about wolfing raw meat when Kosiloff came on deck.

The master stood with his heavy boots planted wide apart, his bushy chin thrust forward, his blue eyes gleaming coldly. Ivan saw that he was angry and supposed it was because he had allowed the crew to sit down and eat. But he did nothing and kept on eating.

"You heathen wolves," Kosiloff snarled. "Eating raw meat like a pack of dogs." He advanced and kicked the piece of raw meat out of Ivan's hands. "I'll flog the next man I catch eating raw meat." He glared about at his crew.

The men tossed the meat overboard and got to their feet. When Kosiloff raged they always made themselves scarce. Ivan got up very slowly.

"Raw meat keeps the scurvy out of a man's system," he said very slowly.

"More of your fool ideas," Kosiloff growled. "There is no truth in it as I shall prove. You heard my order, see that it is obeyed."

Ivan nodded grimly. Perhaps the day would come when

the master would ask him for advice. He would wait for that day.

Kosiloff's wrath was increased by the mate's manner. He stepped forward and caught Ivan by the arm. Ivan was not a small man and he was strong, in a lean wiry way, but Kosiloff's grip made him cringe. The master's thick fingers sank into his arm, and with a jerk Ivan was swung around. Kosiloff's fist shot out and the blow caught the other below the ear. He went down as though shot, slumping into a limp heap on the deck. Kosiloff looked down at his mate and his beard parted in a smile.

"My fine boy, you have not learned much, but you will learn."

Ivan rolled over and sat up, his eyes glassy and out of focus. He shook his head and got slowly to his feet. When he had steadied himself he made an effort to clear the fog out of his head so that he could meet the master's gaze.

"Tomorrow we land and go to the village. We will take aboard a crew of hunters and a number of boats, then we will find new hunting grounds." His eyes bored into Ivan as he waited for the mate's reply.

"Yes, sir," Ivan said, and now his eyes had cleared so that he could meet Kosiloff's gaze.

The master stared at his mate for a full minute before turning away. His fury increased as he saw that Ivan had not been cowed by the lesson he had received; he was still coldly defiant, even though he did say "yes, sir" and agree.

Ivan went below and sat down on his bunk. Several of the Cossacks had seen him knocked down. They grinned as the mate seated himself. The cabin was small and filthy, smelling of bilge water and other rank odors. Ivan looked about, meeting the eyes of each man. Under his cold gaze the smiles vanished and the men turned away from him.

Sometimes they feared Ivan more than they did the master.

Kosiloff retired to his little cabin. He sat down and pulled out his record books. Slowly he went over the figures he had entered. His red beard parted in a hungry smile as he tallied up the number of otter skins he had stored in the hold. The expedition was a co-operative adventure. Kosiloff set down the total figure, then divided it according to the written paper which had been filled out before leaving port. First the catch would be divided equally, one half going to the merchants who had built the *Petr*, one half being again divided between himself and the crew. He would take a rourth of the whole catch, one half of the share left after the owners had received their part. Then the Imperial Russian governor would receive a tenth part of the share of each. The Russian church would receive a share, too. Even then Kosiloff would be wealthy and the men would earn enough to keep them idle and drunk for many months. Kosiloff folded the tally sheets and shoved them into a leather case. Perhaps one of the crew would not receive his share. Ivan was a stubborn fool and did not deserve to get back home at all. He had once lived among the savages and might again have to seek shelter with them. When he was no longer useful Kosiloff could put him ashore and leave him.

Leaning back, the master let his thoughts wander. He would build a ship of his own and a castle where he could gather a band of tough and hardy men around him who would serve as his crew. Having his own ship would do away with the need for surrendering half of each catch, and having a band of fighting men would make him independent and powerful.

Behind Kosiloff, in a wide rack, stood the muskets and heavy swords which were the armament of the *Petr*. Kosiloff kept the arms and the powder and ball locked in his cabin, to be issued as needed. He took no chances with his crew.

A desire to celebrate his great good fortune came upon him and he shouted out to the cook's galley for wine and hot food. While he waited he lolled back with his eyes closed and let plans build themselves into dreams.

14. PRISONER

Kosiloff appeared at the village at the head of a band of armed men. The sea-hunters were outside their huts waiting. Metek stood beside Kagia. The Aleuts were silent and grim. Ivan stepped forward to deliver Kosiloff's orders.

"The master will take ten bidarkas and twenty-four men," he said. "They will come at once."

One of the old men stepped forward and spoke. "The time of the storms and the snow is very near, perhaps it will come tomorrow, perhaps tonight. Then will come the ice and there will be no hunting. The men would wait until summer comes again."

Ivan translated this message for the master. Kosiloff scowled. He answered gruffly, "Tell them that unless twenty-four men march down to the beach at once I will order my men to fire upon the village."

Ivan delivered this ultimatum and the Aleuts began talking in low tones. None of them had weapons and they were considering the fate that would come upon them if they resisted. They would be killed, they were certain, and then what would happen to the women and children? One of the hunters stepped forward, and without looking at his

137

companions, started down toward the beach. Others followed. Kagia was the second to go. Metek saw that the young men without wives and children were offering themselves. He hurried after Kagia.

"Get your harpoons and lances," Ivan shouted after them.

"They are in the boats," one of the hunters answered.

The bidarkas danced out across the bay with two boats from the *Petr* following them closely. High, white-capped seas came rolling in from the ocean to meet them. A black wall of fog moved slowly in from the stormy water outside the sheltered harbor and the wind screamed above the cliffs. By the time the bidarkas had reached the ship, snow was swirling down into the waves and the water looked black. Kosiloff stood in the bow of the leading boat and looked out to sea. Ivan sat behind him waiting for his orders. The master shrugged his shoulders.

"Take the bidarkas aboard," he ordered. "Herd the savages forward."

Ivan took command while Kosiloff went on deck. The bidarkas were loaded and the sea-hunters were herded forward where they squatted upon the bare deck with the wind whipping around them. Ivan stood looking down at the hunters, then he turned to Metek, who had remained standing.

"Can they stay out here in a storm and not freeze?" he asked.

"I think not," Metek replied.

Ivan turned away and went to Kosiloff's cabin. He pounded upon the door and the heavy voice of the master answered, "Come."

Ivan entered and stood before Kosiloff. "A storm is blowing up, sir. I believe the savages will all perish unless we put them below or build a shelter for them."

For a long minute Kosiloff studied his mate. When he spoke it was in a harsh voice. "They will not freeze, and if they do we can replace them."

"You will not build a shelter for them?"

"No." Kosiloff's eyes glittered in the yellow light from the sperm-oil lamp swinging in its gimbals. "Get on deck and prepare to put out to sea. Follow the coast west."

Ivan's gaze did not shift from the master's face. His expression did not change. He would not argue any more, though he knew Kosiloff was making a foolish move. He turned about and left the cabin.

On deck he began shouting orders. The crew swarmed up from below decks and stood in surly silence while he gave orders to weigh anchor and spread canvas. Ivan finished with the crisp statement, "Those are the orders of Kosiloff."

The men growled, but when Ivan reached for a heavy stave they scattered to their work. The *Petr* was soon running fast, her masts groaning, a howling gale ripping through the rigging and whipping the small sails, which were all the burden she could carry. Ivan crouched into the wind, his eyes almost closed against the stinging sleet.

"Rocks, broad on the lee bow!" a Cossack shouted.

"Keep her away two points," Ivan bellowed, cupping his hands to his mouth and thrusting his body forward toward the man at the helm.

"Steady!" shouted the snow-enveloped helmsman.

The *Petr* wallowed and plunged, creaking in every joint, her deck planking opening and closing under the strain. Gradually the black rocks fell abeam of the ship, but there was no seeing what was ahead, so thick was the storm. Ivan stirred himself and sent lookout men to the jibboom end, foreyardarms and several other places. The *Petr* would have to feel her way carefully out of the bay.

The *Petr* wallowed slowly out into the open sea, fighting the great waves, sinking and rising, plunging into the green mountains of water. The hissing spray swept over her deck and drenched the sea-hunters as they huddled forward. They had pulled their bidarkas around them and the frail boats gave some protection from the lashing waves and the sheets of sleet.

Metek was uncomfortable, his hands and feet chilled, but he shared none of the fears of Ivan and the Cossack sailors; he was certain the great ship could not be harmed by wind or waves. To him, the *Petr* was a living monster, master of the sea. The other hunters crouched beside him and no one spoke.

Kosiloff came on deck, roused by the pitching of the ship and the fury of the storm. He fought his way to Ivan's side and gripped the forecastle deck rail.

"It blows a hurricane!" Ivan bellowed to the master.

"It does," Kosiloff shouted back, and Ivan could see that his red beard was parted in a smile. "But we have weathered worse and there is no chance to loosen canvas without having it ripped to ribbons. If she does not wear, loosen sail."

Ivan grunted. Any attempt to send men into the rigging would mean the loss of some of the crew. Kosiloff did not seem greatly disturbed. He was looking down at the sea-hunters huddled upon the deck. Already ice was forming on everything, even upon the fur clothing of the Aleuts. Kosiloff growled an order that made Ivan jerk about.

"If the ice keeps fastening upon those savages dump them and their boats over the side."

"I can't fill an order like that," Ivan answered. "Do it yourself, sir."

"You'll do it, but there is no hurry. It may be the storm will break and we can use them if they are not all frozen stiff." Kosiloff laughed into the teeth of the wind. This was his first arctic voyage and he was meeting forces that challenged his stubborn nature.

Very suddenly the wind shifted to northeast and the ship pitched and plunged. Ivan bellowed to his master.

"This wind will drive us straight against the peninsula."

"I think not. Run with it and we will find a channel," Kosiloff shouted.

Swaying, clinging to the rail, Ivan peered at Kosiloff. The master was smiling and undisturbed. Ivan fought his way to the deck and began putting the *Petr* about so that she heeled down wind. He peered ahead into the flying mass of whiteness, certain that at any moment breakers would show ahead.

The breakers did not show and the *Petr* raced along with the gale howling around her. Ivan stopped to see how the hunters were getting on. He was convinced they would lose every man unless he sent them below. He was about to give Metek orders to lead them into the hold when the ship slipped under the lee of a row of towering cliffs which dropped abruptly into deep water. The helmsman was shouting and the Cossacks were working to keep the *Petr* from smashing into the gray wall of rock. Ivan smiled and bent down, shouting to the Aleuts.

Numbly the men scrambled to their feet. Ivan made off to have the ship stand by long enough for the Aleuts to unload. He came back as the sea-hunters were going over the side, unmindful of the danger, eager to escape. He caught Metek by the arm.

"I need you, you stay with me."

Metek watched the Aleuts tumble and slide over the side. One bidarka was swamped and as it swept out of sight he could see two men clinging to its frail shell. Others managed to get into their boats and head for the high cliffs. Metek never knew how many reached safety, but he was certain a number were lost. He followed Ivan aft and waited for orders.

Before Ivan and his crew could take advantage of the haven under the cliffs, the *Petr* was out in the gale again and had to stand away from the line of cliffs or be smashed against their walls. Kosiloff came forward and bellowed at Ivan.

"You slow-witted fool, why didn't you put in under those cliffs?"

"I did my best, sir," Ivan answered.

"Do you know that we're being driven into the northern seas where few have gone?" Kosiloff demanded. "We'll find no otter in such a waste."

"I think we are heading into the sea Bering so recently discovered," Ivan said. "I will quarter and run west if you say so."

Kosiloff caught the irony of the remark. The *Petr* was barely able to keep afloat running down wind with the storm; to put her into a fight, with the seas rolling over her decks, would most certainly swamp her. He glared at Ivan.

"You'd do just that," he said slowly. "But we're running with the gale until it blows itself out."

"Yes, sir," Ivan agreed.

"And why did you leave this savage when you unloaded the others?" Kosiloff demanded.

"I can use this boy. He knows the north because he is an Innuit, not a sea-hunter," Ivan replied.

Kosiloff bent toward Metek and stared hard at him. "He seems a bright one. Send him to help the cook. He's been kicking for a scullery rat ever since we left port."

Ivan nodded. "Aye, sir," he said and turned to Metek. "You'll go with me."

The galley filled the entire space between the forehatch and the mainmast, and with every heavy sea that smashed over the deck a flood descended upon the cook's quarters. Kosiloff's cabin occupied a space some six by ten feet in the after half of the trunk, which extended two feet above the quarter-deck. Two bull's-eyes gave feeble light for the master's quarters by day. The men's quarters were under the forecastle deck, close against the deadwood of the ship's eyes. Metek stared at everything. To him the cabins and the galley were commodious quarters equipped with numerous interesting things.

The cook was slopping up sea water and mumbling curses upon the weather when Ivan brought Metek into the galley. The fire had escaped drenching and a great pot of stew filled the cabin with appetizing odors. The cook straightened from his work and turned around to glare at his visitors.

"Vatchel, this is your new flunky but he speaks no Russian," Ivan said.

Vatchel was a short man with a stomach that protruded like a sack of cabbage and seemed to be held in place by the hemp rope knotted around his waist. He had a massive head with no hair visible though his greasy cap was shoved far back. His little eyes twinkled deep in his fat face and his double chin rolled when he spoke.

"So! Kosiloff sends me a heathen when I ask for a man." He clamped his big, red hands upon his hips and his stomach rolled with the lurch of the ship.

"Show some patience and he will learn," Ivan said sourly.

"Patience!" Vatchel caught up a meat-ax and sunk the blade into the chopping block. "Who has time for patience when this blasted ship is floundering. Not one among all of you could sail a scallop on a calm sea. You fill my galley with dirty sea water. At any moment we may expect to go to the bottom." He shook a fist at Ivan.

"Nevertheless I'd advise you to have that hot scum ready for the men or they may throw you over the side," Ivan warned. "And do not abuse the boy."

"I will cut his head off and toss it into your stew if he so much as steps behind me. I'll have no heathen leaping upon my back. I trust no raw-meat-gnawing wild men." Vatchel turned his gaze upon the frightened Metek.

"He shouts very loud like a dog barking but he has never bitten anyone," Ivan explained in broken Innuit.

Metek smiled but he did not take his eyes off the fat face of the cook.

"See! He grins like a fiend up to tricks!" Vatchel shouted.

At that moment an unusually heavy sea hit the *Petr* and she reeled. A sheet of water descended into the galley swirling around Metek and sending him staggering against the cook. They both went down and Vatchel would have remained with his head under a bench if Metek had not laid hold upon him and dragged him out. The cook staggered up with Metek's help. He shook his head and glowered about him. The fire was out but the kettle of stew was safe because it had a wooden cover which fitted tight except for a steam hole in the top.

"Get to that bucket and clear out the water," Vatchel growled as he kicked a bucket toward Metek. He had softened considerably because Metek had rescued him from a bad spot.

Metek understood and set to work while the cook raked out the soggy coals and began rebuilding the fire to make coffee. After an hour it became evident that the ship was riding more smoothly. She still groaned in every timber and swayed sickeningly but she was not shipping much water. Listening to the storm, Metek knew it had settled down to a steady gale which would, quite likely, blow for several days.

Vatchel, now that his galley was fairly dry underfoot, had regained his fat-man's good humor. There was a twinkle in his little eyes as he ladled out the stew and slid a wooden bowl of it along the table to Metek.

"Get that inside you," he said, tossing Metek a wooden spoon. "I want to see if it is good enough for those swine on deck."

Metek hesitated, then fell to eating, using the spoon so awkwardly that the cook roared and slapped a fat leg. In an amazingly short time Metek emptied the bowl. Vatchel grunted as he refilled it. Metek ate all of the second helping. The cook eyed him suspiciously.

"I'll bet the Empress's jewels against a bag of bones that varmint-skinning pirate, Kosiloff, hasn't been feeding you anything at all." He refilled the bowl and shoved it along the table.

Metek finished the third bowl, and now the cook was amazed but determined to see how much this heathen could eat. He knew nothing about Eskimos and their capacity for food. A fourth bowl was emptied but Metek could eat no more though he would have liked to please the grinning white man.

Ivan appeared in the companionway demanding hot food and coffee for the men. Vatchel turned upon him.

"This young 'un has some big stomach," he said with a grin. "He has eaten the rations of four men. But see, he is not fat like me."

Ivan laughed. "You should see his people eat up a whole walrus at one meal and raw at that."

"He'll eat no raw meat here," the cook said grimly. "I'll have no such heathen thing going on in my galley."

"You may eat raw meat and like it," Ivan answered. "Raw meat has its place when you're iced in."

The cook and Metek carried the kettle to the cabin where a broken skylight had allowed much sea water to pour over the rough table. The men were gathered around armed with wooden spoons and bowls for the steaming mixture which passed for coffee. Kosiloff came down and issued rum which the men poured into their coffee, then gulped the scalding liquid down in great draughts. After drinking, they attacked the stew, ladling it out with the big spoons and wolfing it down. After they had eaten as much as was needed to take the edge off their hunger they dipped hard cask-bread into the stew and wiped the kettle clean.

Ivan explained to Metek that he was to remain and carry the kettle and the wooden spoons and bowls back to the galley. Metek squatted beside the companionway and watched every move the sailors made.

Later that night Vatchel made a place for him in the galley and he rolled up in his robe which the cook allowed him to dry before the fire. Vatchel had a bunk off the cook's galley in a small space which he shared with two barrels of flour, the stovepipe and the steward's pantry. Metek fell asleep at once with the roar of the storm in his ears. For the first time since he had feasted upon whale, his stomach was bursting full and that called for sleep.

15. ICEBLINK

After a few days it became evident that the *Petr* would ride out the storm, though she could do little to shape her own course. Ivan admitted he was lost and Kosiloff raged about for hours, abusing his mate and his crew. He might have dealt severely with Ivan but for the fact that he was the only man among his ill-trained band who knew anything at all about the northern wastes into which they were heeling like a scudding gull. Kosiloff had never sailed a ship except in coastwise trade where landmarks were always at hand. Plunging through icy waters with fog and pelting snow swirling around the ship, with only the white crests of the rushing seas in view and those visible only for a few yards around the bridge, Kosiloff was willing to let Ivan handle the ship.

Metek sniffed the chill wind and tasted the stinging sleet. He smiled broadly because the course they were following would surely take him home. The *Petr* finally scudded into the Bering Strait. Luckily she picked a course east of the Diomedes but close enough so that Ivan, standing upon the bridge, heard the roar of the surf upon the nearer of the two rocky islands standing midway in the channel. He held his men ready to work ship but no breakers showed ahead and the roaring died away.

147

And so the *Petr* sailed swiftly into the icy waters of the
Arctic Ocean without her crew or her master knowing
she had slipped through the narrows discovered by Vitus
Jonassen Bering a few years before. The current of the
ocean-river carried the ship faster than she had been traveling before, sweeping her into the unknown polar basin.

A day later the storm raced on leaving the *Petr* crawling
along under small sails with a brisk wind at her back. The
clouds raced away on the tail of the gale and the fog lifted.
The crew of the *Petr* looked out upon a chill expanse of
gray-green water with no trace of land in any direction.
The stolid calm and the intrepid nature of the Russian,
which is so little understood by other peoples, was shown
by the manner in which master and crew met the problem.
They were lost in an unknown ocean, their ship was badly
shaken and in no condition to face another gale. Kosiloff
turned to Ivan.

"Put about. We will return over our course."

"Aye, sir," Ivan answered. As he spoke his eyes were
fixed upon dancing lights blinking to the westward. He
turned to the crew and shouted orders. "Heave away!"

"Aye, aye, sir!" shouted a Cossack and the men set to
work. As the men toiled in the rigging the wind began to
freshen and blow in squalls. The ship was put about and
she began working south and east.

Within two hours, a heavy line of icebergs was seen
lying across the ship's course. Ivan was not surprised; he
had already noted the blink of the sun from their spires.
Their forms were as various as their dimensions, from solid
wall-sided masses of dead white, to old weather-worn
Gothic spires whose crystal peaks melted into the blue sky.
They seemed to be endless and numberless, and so close
together that no passage could be seen.

The wind had suddenly died to a mere cat's-paw and

the ship ceased to make headway of its own but simply drifted toward the wall of ice. The bergs, influenced only by the undercurrents, were to the anxious watchers on the deck practically stationary, and the surface current which was guiding the ship, as she lost her steerageway, made her position anything but safe. Ivan made ready to meet the emergency.

The *Petr* met the line of bergs and sidled against a towering mountain of ice, which presented a jagged, honeycombed appearance indicative of its great age. Ivan watched anxiously, giving orders to the men to be ready with poles to shove the ship away should she decide to snuggle against the old berg. Such a berg was a dangerous neighbor, because the least disturbance of its equilibrium might cause the whole mass to crumble to pieces. In such an event the *Petr* would be smashed like matchwood.

The ship idled past the old berg and came alongside a table of ice. The ice poles were put to work and the course of the ship was changed. Even the toughened Cossacks grinned with relief as the *Petr* sheered away. In a moment they were plunged into danger again as an eddy caught the ship and sent her right back against the ancient monster they had just passed. The *Petr* revolved slowly in the current and headed straight for the old one. She touched on the starboard quarter, and the shock, though slight, loosened fragments of ice that would have smashed the vessel had they struck her. A shower of smaller lumps rattled down upon the deck. The quarter-deck was quickly cleared and all hands crowded forward to watch the ship. Slowly the berg began to revolve, settling over the *Petr* like a great monster crouching for a leap upon its prey. Slowly the ice descended upon the afterdeck, and the forecastle was the only place of safety. Suddenly an immense mass broke away from that part which was beneath the surface of the sea, and this, ten times bigger than the ship, came rushing up a few yards from her, sending foaming torrents of water spouting into the air.

The breaking away of this piece stopped the revolving of the berg and it began settling in the opposite direction, but another danger soon appeared. A long tongue of ice was sticking out from the berg directly under the ship. Already the keel was slipping and grinding upon it, and it seemed certain the *Petr* would be tossed into the air or capsized. The ship rose and the deck took a steep incline. Feverishly the Cossacks worked with ice poles in an attempt to shove the *Petr* off the ice prong which was thrusting at her bottom. The men made no headway at all, but they did not cease pushing.

Suddenly a loud report broke the silence, followed by another and another, until the air was filled with roaring like that of cannons. The far side of the berg had slipped away. Piece after piece plunged into the sea, each with a hissing roar. The berg shuddered, then began to revolve slowly again. The Cossacks, their white faces turned up toward the ice swaying above them again threatening the deck, strained at the ice poles wildly, momentarily expecting the whole side nearest them to break loose and crash bodily upon the ship, carrying her down like a trapper's hut before a landslide.

By this time Ivan had succeeded in planting an ice anchor. His voice rang out. "Haul in!"

The Cossacks leaped to grasp the rope and pulled with all their strength. Even Kosiloff laid hold and pulled, while Metek and Vatchel added their strength. Slowly the *Petr* moved off. The seconds seemed like hours to the straining men. Slowly and steadily the berg behind them sank, carrying away the main boom and grinding hard against the quarter. But the *Petr* had escaped. She was twenty yards away when the crew turned to watch the total destruction of the berg. The whole half of the mountain nearest the ship split off and plunged into the sea, sending a shower of ice and spray over the deck, drenching the men and raising a swell which set the *Petr* rocking as if in a gale of wind and left her grinding in the debris of the crumbled.ruin.

Even after the *Petr* had moved far enough away to be clear of any danger, the remaining portion of the berg rocked and rolled like a thing alive. At each movement, fresh masses of ice were loosened and plunged hissing into the foaming sea. After several hours it settled down and floated, only a fragment of its former greatness, among the broken pieces that had once been its towers and spires.

The scene was one of great beauty, though none aboard the *Petr* was in a mood to enjoy it. The heavens were a mass of rich, warm color, the sea like a rainbow, dissolved into a sheet of color, with the flaming bergs floating upon it. Later the sky became gray, the air clear, and the ice everywhere turned dead white or cold, transparent blue.

Ivan ordered most of the crew below to rest. He sent Vatchel and Metek to the galley to prepare a hot meal while he remained on deck with four sailors. Kosiloff returned to his cabin in a sulky mood, angered because of the ill-luck which dogged his course.

Vatchel had formed a habit of talking to Metek. He was by nature a man who liked to talk, and that was his main reason for demanding a helper in the galley. Metek had already learned many Russian words. But mostly he could not follow the talk of the cook; he just grinned and nodded his head, always listening curiously.

"The next time," said the cook, as he poised a big slab of rhytina steak over the kettle, "we will not have such good luck. My feet have been cold in my bunk for three

nights, and that is a sign we will not have easy sailing."
He dropped the piece of meat into the kettle.

Metek nodded his head and spoke the only word he had
learned so far. "Good."

"You think that good?" the cook demanded. "Perhaps
it is as good as we deserve."

Again Metek nodded.

"I must teach you some words so that you can tell me
what manner of place this is where mountains of ice float
about." The cook stirred the stew and sniffed as steam rose
out of the kettle.

After a few hours of resting the crew was turned out by
orders from Kosiloff and Ivan set a course eastward along
an open lane of water. Kosiloff had hopes of locating a
lane which would lead through the pack of bergs and allow
the *Petr* to escape. Within five hours the slight breeze died
down and the ship rolled lazily. Ivan stayed on deck because he was certain such a calm could not last very long.
When the wind came it would most certainly be heavy and
the ice would start moving. If luck favored them a lane
would be opened to the south.

Metek, his work in the galley finished, was on deck
watching the sea. Ivan called him over.

"Would you say there was land near?" he asked.

Metek looked at the low-riding sun and nodded. He
pointed northeast. "That way I think," he said.

"Why?" Ivan persisted.

"The way the birds fly," Metek answered. "I think they
fly from land."

"And these bergs, did you ever see big icebergs like
these where you hunted?" Ivan asked.

"No, I think they come from far away," Metek replied.

Ivan nodded. He thought the same thing. The big bergs
came from glaciers sliding down the mountains and not

from the low-lying shores to the north which he had visited when he was shipwrecked and stayed with the Innuits.

"We could kill walrus," Metek said. "We could take the gun that kills with fire and get fresh meat."

Ivan laughed. "We could if Kosiloff would let us, but he will not give anyone a gun or allow anyone to lower a boat."

Around them upon the ice rafts were many walrus and seals. Metek was hungry for fresh meat, raw meat. The salted food was beginning to make him feel queer in the stomach.

Ivan moved aft and Metek went on gazing out across the sea. Within an hour the ship entered new floes. She rammed her way through several fields of the young ice before she was halted by a heavy table some ten feet in thickness. Ivan ordered the ice poles and an attempt was made to free her but she stuck fast. Kosiloff came on deck and stamped about fuming and shouting. Finally he retired to his cabin, leaving the ship's control to Ivan. Night came with the *Petr* firmly held by the ice.

The next morning the crew discovered that the *Petr* was frozen in. Ivan took a dead reckoning and discovered that the entire pack, some forty acres of ice, was drifting north and east. This was very disturbing, being carried deeper into the unknown sea, but there was nothing that could be done about it.

Metek would have climbed down upon the ice for a run but Ivan refused to allow him to leave the ship. He was grimly watching an iceblink which had developed to the northward. Soon a great floe was seen moving slowly eastward across their course. The men on deck lined up along the rail and all watched in silence as the small ice field, which held them trapped, smashed into the endless mass. Welded together, the whole floe began moving east.

The constant pressure of the old ice cracked the young floes. There was distant thundering of heavy masses as they threw up high ridges of young ice, forming valleys and dykes. At intervals of a moment's duration the ice would open near the ship and vast columns of vapor would rise into the cold air. The temperature had dropped sharply and the air was stinging cold. Metek got his parka from the galley where he had left it when Vatchel had insisted that he shed the fur garment while working. The biting wind and the warmth of the parka made him feel at home. He stayed on deck as much as he could.

Two days later a real winter storm swept down out of the north and piled the ice fields high with snow. Bitter cold came with the storm and the Cossacks shuddered and danced about when on deck. The snow afforded fresh water—and that was something to be thankful for—but it added to the discomforts of the men. Metek enjoyed it because he was dressed for such weather. Alternately for ten days the snow came and the wind blew. When the snow ceased the gales swept across the ice and the movement of the floe was great. When the gales slackened to heavy gusts, the snow came. Ivan rigged canvas sheltering for the deck and did what he could to protect the crew from the severe weather. Kosiloff stayed close to his cabin nursing a cold wrath at the fate which had upset his plans.

On the eleventh day, there was tremendous pressure and the floes actually backed up into mounds under the strain. The heaviest stress came in the stem of the ship, in a longitudinal direction. There was also a heavy lateral strain, especially under the starboard main-chains. One of the Cossacks came up from below and reported that water was a foot deep over the floor plates. Ivan set the men to clearing the water away and finding the leak. It was soon discovered that the forefoot had been twisted to starboard.

The carpenter, a Siberian woodsman who was skillful with an ax, but who knew very little about shipbuilding, managed to lessen the leakage. Most of the ship's stock of flour was soaked with salt water.

The weather cleared for a day, and Metek's sharp eyes caught the outline of a low, rolling coast to the eastward. He recognized the round hill formations, which were like the country near his home. He rushed to Ivan and they looked long at the distant coast. There was a lane of blue water between the ice fields and the shore but escape from the *Petr* was possible. The light boats could be dragged across the ice. Ivan went at once to Kosiloff.

The master listened while Ivan talked of escape. When the mate had finished he scowled and said, "We have a fortune in kalan skins in the hold. I do not intend to abandon ship. We will winter on board and when spring comes we will be released and sail home."

"We will be smashed long before spring comes," Ivan said.

"We have lived through so far and will not be smashed now," Kosiloff answered.

Ivan returned to the deck where he stood for a long time looking toward the distant shore. He was certain the fortune in the hold of the *Petr* meant little, that it was bound to be lost. It seemed to him that the most important thing was to save the crew from being driven out on the ice should the *Petr* be smashed. Even if they stayed on board, and the ship was not lost, they faced starvation and scurvy. Ivan knew that soon the walrus and the seals would disappear, that the open lanes of water would close and the long polar night would settle. But he was not willing to disobey his master, so he went to the galley to inspect the evening meal.

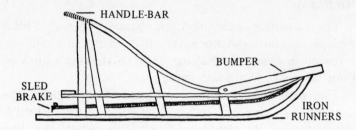

16. THE LONG NIGHT

The *Petr* was firmly embedded in ice about eight feet in thickness, but there were immense masses shoved under her keel, so that the bows were lifted and the keel was inclined about one or two degrees, the ship at the same time heeling to starboard some two or three degrees. The ice was piled under the main-chains as high as the plank-sheer. All around the *Petr* the ice was tumbled in the greatest confusion, and traveling over it was almost impossible.

Kosiloff bestirred himself when he finally realized that all hope of escape was gone until the breakup came many months later. Ivan set to work preparing the ship for winter. She was banked up with snow and a deck house was built for the use of the men. This was constructed of canvas and covered over completely with snow. A whale oil stove was set up for heat and the crew moved up to their new quarters.

Ivan checked the food supplies and the casks of whale oil, which was the only fuel on board. Now that their captivity was certain, Kosiloff ordered parties to set out on hunting trips. The men went out and returned half-frozen and discouraged. They found no open water within walking distance because the northern fields had smashed into the great floe in which they were embedded and had pressed the entire field firmly together. No longer could they see the shore line or the open lane of water Metek had sighted.

The hunting parties were ill-clad, being dressed for service on shipboard in summer weather. The oiled coats used for rain were of no value at all and the cloth coats and undergarments failed to keep out the wind. It was only when the air was still that the hunters could go far across the ice. Ivan watched anxiously for signs of scurvy, the dreaded disease of the north. As the weeks passed he noted a stiffness in many of the men and could feel pains in his own joints. He was certain that trouble would soon be upon them.

In the galley Metek was getting on well with Vatchel. He was learning Russian, chiefly by being a very good listener. The cook took a fancy to the boy. He was glad Ivan had sent him instead of a surly and silent Cossack who would never have been a good listener.

Metek liked the fat cook. He learned words eagerly and listened wide-eyed to the stories Vatchel told. They concerned his own exploits mostly, but this was what Metek would have expected because among his own people a story-teller always described his own adventures. Always his yarns were about lands far to the south where there was warmth and sunshine and green, growing things.

The China markets, visited on trading voyages, were his favorites. Seated upon a stool with Metek sitting upon the planking looking up at him, Vatchel would describe the China ports and the people.

"Those yellow men are too dumb to sail out of sight of land but they make all manner of things." Vatchel tugged at his beard with long, white fingers that always fascinated Metek. Then he would add, after saying the Chinese were dumb, "But it may be they are wise to let the fool Russians risk the sea to get furs and whale oil and ivory, while they sit at home and weave colored cloth and make things in their shops. They trade for what the sea has to give without braving her dangers."

Metek would agree that the Chinese were, perhaps, very wise people.

"I would go to the China ports and see," he would say.

"When we break loose from this frozen cellar of darkness and sail south, I will take you," Vatchel promised.

And as they drifted slowly northward darkness came. One day the sun hung low above the ice pack; the next it glowed behind the spires, and after that there was only a radiance in the sky. When that radiance faded, there was starlight and moonlight. The faces of the white men became pasty-white like potato sprouts growing in a dark cellar. Vatchel grumbled and kept Metek close to the galley for company. Having the boy to talk to made the hours pass more quickly.

And every meal was the same, salt-meat stew with salt-water-soaked flour added. The bread casks were emptied and the rum supply was very low, so that it had to be rationed as medicine. Metek was ravenous for fresh, raw meat and often spoke to the cook about it. Vatchel was still horrified at the thought of eating raw meat and lectured Metek every time he mentioned it, and as for drinking blood, he became wild in his denunciations when Metek told how fine it was for one's health.

Ivan headed many parties out on the ice. He had fixed himself a fur outfit such as he had known while among the Innuits and was able to travel in more comfort than the others. One day he went to Kosiloff. The master listened to his mate sourly.

"We should outfit at least six men with fur clothing, then we could travel far enough to find open water and walrus," he said.

"Where will you get the furs?" Kosiloff asked.

"We have hundreds of kalan skins," Ivan reminded him.

"Dress those dogs in the robes of kings? Put fur outfits worth three thousand silver rubles a suit on their dirty backs?" Kosiloff burst into a deep laugh and brought his hairy fist down upon the table before him. "No!" he roared. "Let the sniveling dogs freeze stiff."

Ivan looked at him without any trace of feeling showing on his face. "Those kalan pelts mean much to you, sir," he said slowly.

"They do and every last one of them is to be sold for the highest price it will bring. Not one pelt will be cut up to cover the back of a lousy sailor." Kosiloff glowered at his mate. "Now get out of here."

"Then I will take the Innuit boy and we will hunt. But we must have guns," Ivan said boldly.

Kosiloff smoothed his red beard and his tongue ran along his lips, back and forth. His stomach was revolting at Vatchel's salt-meat stews, and the supply of preserved things stored in his locker was very low. After a moment's consideration, he got to his feet and took two muskets from the rack on the wall. He handed the guns to Ivan along with powder and ball.

"See that you keep them always under your care," he said gruffly, "and bring in some fresh meat."

Ivan hurried away and a moment later entered the galley. Vatchel stared at the guns, then heaved his bulk up from the bench where he had been sitting. A twinge of pain twisted his face and he rubbed his knees.

"Did you steal those guns?" he demanded.

"No. The master gave them to me. I am taking your boy and we are going hunting," Ivan explained.

Metek leaped to his feet eagerly. Vatchel grunted sourly. "I need him here," he said. "My joints are so sore and stiff that if I do not have help there'll be no food cooked for the crew."

"A rest from your slops would help their stomachs," Ivan said and grinned widely.

"So!" Vatchel waddled toward the chopping block and jerked the meat ax from it. "So!" he rumbled. "You come here to insult me."

"I come to take the boy." Ivan turned to Metek. "Get your fur clothing. We start on a hunt." He faced the cook. "I will send you one, two, or more men to help with your rotten stews."

"Send one man," Vatchel said.

"We will bring fresh meat and the meat will cure the sickness in you," Metek said eagerly.

"There is no cure. It is the curse that comes to us because of what we have done," Vatchel said. But he added, "Bring me a fine, fat steak, son, I could eat such a one."

Ivan and Metek made ready for a hunt. Metek brought his sleeping robe; then they went to the carpenter who fashioned a rude sled according to the directions of the two hunters. When it was finished Metek thought it a very fine sled but Ivan doubted if it would hang together at all. They wrapped the guns up in the bed robe along with a lamp, some oil, Metek's harpoon, and a slab of salted sea cow.

Sliding down the snowbank which was piled against the ship they set off into the starlight. Ivan allowed Metek to set their course. When they were far out on the ice, they halted and Ivan seated himself. He ordered Metek to unwrap the guns and they spent an hour while Ivan instructed Metek in loading and firing the musket.

Metek's forehead was beaded with sweat and his whole body was trembling the first time he pressed the trigger, and when the musket roared and smoke and flame belched from its muzzle he dropped the gun and would have dashed away, but that Ivan caught and held him. He showed Metek

where the ball had struck, a full five feet from the patch of
seaweed they had used as a target.

"You must hold it firmly when you press the trigger.
All the time you are pressing you must keep your sight
steady. If you jerk and close your eyes you will hit nothing," Ivan explained.

"The little killer follows the eyes?" Metek asked.

"Yes," Ivan answered solemnly. "The ball goes fast along
the light from your eye."

Metek nodded and from then on he did not miss, though
he always cringed when he pressed the trigger.

They repacked the sled and moved on, always straining
their eyes for open water. Finally Metek sighted a little
snow-dog. Ivan did not see the white one at all.

"There, by that block of ice, watching us," Metek whispered

"Shoot it," Ivan said. "I do not see anything."

Metek took careful aim and fired. The fox bounded
into the air and fell dead. Metek rushed forward eagerly,
with Ivan close upon his heels. They sat down and Metek
got out his knife. In a moment he had stripped the pelt
away, saving the tail for a windbreaker. He cut away a
portion of the saddle and handed it to Ivan, then sliced
off a piece for himself.

They sat on a slab of ice and devoured the whole carcass. When they had finished, Ivan laughed.

"Kosiloff would clap us in irons if he could see us wolfing raw meat."

"Vatchel would be so very angry. Do you think he will
smell the raw meat I have eaten?" Metek asked.

"No matter. We will escape the scurvy if we eat raw
meat," Ivan answered. "If the others are so stubborn, there
is nothing we can do about it, but we will not be such fools
ourselves."

They started on across the ice, keeping a sharp watch for bear, or for more of the little snow-dogs. Metek sniffed the air and looked far ahead. He sought open water where walrus and seals would be found.

At last a bitter wind sprang up and blew itself into a gale. Metek halted and Ivan allowed him to dig a burrow into the snow. The white-man's legs and arms were stiff with cold and he knew that, in spite of the fur garments he wore, he would soon freeze. They crawled into the shelter and lay there for hours, sleeping and waking. At last the wind died down and they crawled out to find the stars gleaming brightly upon a world newly carved and shaped by the wind.

During the faint midday glow which marked the nearest to light there would be, Metek sighted a white bear. The great brute was digging among a pile of tumbled ice cakes, evidently trying to uncover a fox which had taken shelter there. Ivan finally saw the white bear, after Metek had whispered and pointed for some minutes.

"We will crawl upon him," Metek said.

"Do not fire until we are very close." Ivan warned. He did not have the limitless faith in the muskets that filled Metek. The Innuit boy was convinced the magic weapons would kill at any range so long as the eye could see the game.

They left the sled and began working to the windward. The bear was so ravenously hungry that it was not watchful. Growling and snarling, it tore away large pieces of ice and tossed them into the air. The hunters were able to approach to within a few yards. Lying flat, they took careful aim and Ivan gave the word to fire. The muskets belched black smoke and fire. With a roar of rage and pain the bear turned half around, backed away, its long neck swaying back and forth as it sought to locate the enemy that had attacked it.

Metek was greatly disappointed because the bear did not fall down dead at once. Ivan halted and began reloading, but Metek caught up his harpoon and leaped forward. He was thrusting at the wounded bear, dancing around the beast, shouting wildly, when Ivan came up and finished the big one with a ball from very close range.

"You should stop at once and reload," Ivan explained.

Metek grinned widely. He was learning the limitations of a black-powder musket. They fell upon the bear and began skinning it and cutting meat to tie to their sled. When they had loaded on all they could haul, they built a cache and covered the remainder with heavy blocks of ice. It would be necessary to make several trips before all of the meat could be dragged to the ship.

The trip back was made in much less time than they had taken in coming out upon the ice. Ivan set marks to guide them back to the cache as they moved along. Strengthened by the fresh liver of the bear, they were able to travel steadily. Ivan finally slowed the pace. He could not hold the steady trot the Innuit boy used when in a hurry.

"We'll walk for a mile or so," he ordered.

"Sure," Metek agreed and settled into a walk.

Kosiloff was surprised when they came aboard. He had decided that they had deserted and made off seeking the mainland. The Cossacks were as excited as they could possibly be over the prospect of fresh meat. Vatchel came near to hugging Metek.

That night there was a feast of roast bear meat. Vatchel would have made a great pot of stew but the men rose up and demanded roast. The cook grumbled and fumed about but he roasted the meat and set it out on two huge platters.

Ivan made an attempt to have some of the flesh served

raw, but Kosiloff would allow none of it to be eaten until it had been cooked a deep brown.

"The Innuits never have swollen gums or stiff joints from scorbutus," Ivan said.

"And so, because of that, we must act like savages," the master growled. "Let me catch no one gnawing bloody flesh."

Ivan shrugged his shoulders and left the cabin. He found Metek busily helping Vatchel in the galley. The men were stirring about sniffing the odor of crisping meat that floated out to their quarters.

When Vatchel and Metek set the platters on the rough table, the men closed in like wolves and fell upon the savory meal. Vatchel carried a platter to Kosiloff's cabin. The master feasted, drinking hot rum and cramming himself with roast. There was no rum for the men, but they did not miss it.

Ivan stood watching them as they gorged themselves. He saw among them unmistakable signs of scurvy. They poured much salt upon their fresh meat, seeming to crave the very thing which was bringing on the dread disease. The gums of many were swollen over their teeth, so that they made painful faces as they chewed the tough bear meat. They were low in spirits and many of them limped from stiffness in the joints. Ivan wondered how long it would be before the crew would be in such bad shape that Kosiloff would listen to him.

After a rest and a sleep, Ivan and Metek set out and brought in another load of meat. Then Ivan spoke bluntly to Kosiloff about the supply.

"The meat must be rationed. We may not have any success at all upon our next hunt. The carcass should be hung in the rigging and guarded carefully."

"Give the orders," Kosiloff answered. He was willing

to take any measures which would help to save food, and he knew the Cossacks would glut themselves if allowed all they could eat.

Ivan set one man in charge of the meat, a fellow he could trust more than any of the others. He could not take charge himself because he had another trip to make before all of the meat was brought in.

It was with satisfaction that the mate noted the condition of himself and the Innuit boy. Neither of them showed any signs of scurvy. On the last trip they got another fox and ate a large part of it raw, bringing the remainder in with them.

The days dragged by slowly, with the condition of the crew growing steadily worse. Kosiloff dosed the men with physic, the only remedy in the ship's medical cabinet. Metek was deeply worried about his friend Vatchel. The cook could scarcely get up from his bench. His face was swollen and his gums red and bloody. But he did not growl and grumble as much as he did when well. Metek talked to him one day after he and Ivan had returned from a three-day hunt which had netted only one fox. Metek had asked Ivan to allow him to save the blood which he had caught in his little pot, and the heart and liver. Metek explained that he wished to take them to Vatchel as medicine.

Standing beside the cook, he smiled down at him. Vatchel tried to smile but his lips were too swollen.

"You look healthy and fit, son," he said. "But with me it is different. Your old, fat friend will never live to see the spring come."

"I can cure you," Metek said simply. "I can cure you the way my people cure themselves."

Vatchel looked at him and for a moment there was a gleam of hope in his dull eyes. Then he said, slowly, "You can do no more for me than Kosiloff with his physic."

Metek produced the little pot. He set it close to the stone stove so that the contents would melt. Then he laid out the frozen heart and liver.

"Will you do as I say?" he asked.

"I will, son," Vatchel said, but he eyed the raw meat with suspicion.

"You see I am well and strong," Metek argued. "I will not be sick because I know the way of this land. It is my land and I have always lived here."

Vatchel nodded and grinned feebly. "You are a wise one for a boy," he said.

Metek took the pot of melted blood. He stepped close to Vatchel. "Drink all of this," he said.

Vatchel looked into the pot and shuddered. "If I were not already a hopeless sinner I would not dare touch it."

"Ever since I was a baby, I have drunk it," Metek urged.

Vatchel gripped the pot and drained it without stopping. When he had finished, he licked his puffed lips and grunted.

"That was a wicked thing," he said. "But it is much better than rum."

Metek laughed happily. He began cutting up the heart and liver. Piece by piece, he fed his friend. Meekly Vatchel ate the flesh. He would have doused it with salt but Metek would not allow it. When the last scrap had vanished, the cook looked up at Metek.

"It is best that you do not tell anyone what medicine you give," he said. "Kosiloff would toss me into the dungeon if he knew about this."

"I say nothing," Metek answered. "Ivan and you and me, we have a secret we will keep."

They both laughed. After that, Vatchel went to his bunk and lay down, the first time he had left his bench in several days. Metek went and found Ivan. He was beaming and happy. They were alone outside the shelter and Metek spoke eagerly.

"I think Vatchel will get well," he said.

"He drank and ate?" Ivan asked with a smile.

"Yes," Metek said. "But we must not tell."

"We will have to face Kosiloff and force a showdown very soon. Everyone will have to use your cure if the crew is to live through," Ivan said grimly.

Metek rolled his eyes. He did not want to have anything to do with telling Kosiloff he must eat raw meat and make his men eat it.

Ivan and Metek hunted steadily for the next six weeks but took very little game. Ivan rationed the fresh meat among the men, but there was never enough to furnish meals without the use of much salted rhytina. One after another, the men came down with scurvy. Kosiloff refused to go to his bunk and stay there. He was constantly prowling around the ship giving orders, growling and bellowing at the men. Patiently Ivan waited, hoping the master would go down, so that he could take charge of the crew.

In the galley, Vatchel was on his feet again and well on the road to complete recovery. He ate the raw meat and drank the blood Metek brought to him, and the boy managed to get a larger share for his friend than was allotted even to himself. Ivan saw plainly that Metek was breaking his rules but he grinned to himself and said nothing. Like Vatchel, he had formed a strong attachment for the young Innuit.

Finally a period of three weeks came when they killed no game at all. One morning Kosiloff did not appear upon deck, and Ivan went to the cabin to see what had happened. He found the master in his bunk. Kosiloff stared up at him out of bloodshot eyes and mumbled between swollen lips.

"Take over, Ivan. Do not destroy a single skin and do not abandon ship. I will rest here for a few days."

"You will take the medicine I give or you will die," Ivan said harshly.

Kosiloff glared up at him out of glassy eyes, his red beard parted, and he laughed.

"I could do well to take some of your medicine. It is plain you and the savage know how to ward off this cursed scurvy." Then he turned over with his face to the wall and refused to speak again.

17. MUTINY

Ivan set to work at once putting his plans into effect. He was master of the *Petr* as long as Kosiloff was held to his bed with stiff joints and swollen muscles. He gave each man definite work to do, anything to keep the crew from sitting still, thinking about themselves. Placing one man in charge on board, he and Metek hunted afield.

The first hunt was a failure, but the second netted a lank, half-starved bear. Ivan issued the men raw meat and saw that they ate it. They grumbled and demanded salt but he would not allow any at all. Standing among them he saw that they finished the portions he had cut for them.

Every day Ivan and Metek issued fresh meat, raw, and the men began to show signs of regaining some of their vigor. Ivan cared for Kosiloff himself. The master was fed some of the blood and much of the liver. Kosiloff did not grumble, but he ate the raw meat with evident distaste.

Metek hunted alone, roving far from the ship, staying out two or three days at a time. He could have headed toward the distant shore which he had discovered lay to the east and south. He had the gun he had wanted to take back to his village; he had powder and ball. But he would not leave his two friends. He had a feeling they would need his help. He managed to locate a seal hole and speared the seal. Ivan's praise made Metek glow and he was as happy as Karsuk had always been when patted.

On the boat the crew was growing strong and it seemed certain they would all shake off the dreaded scurvy. Vatchel was fat and good-natured again. He waddled about the galley humming Russian songs. Kosiloff recovered slowly. Only after three weeks of lying on his back did he begin to sit up. He came on deck a week later and prowled about but gave no orders. Ivan was worried about him and asked him to go back to his cabin, out of the crew's draughty shelter, but Kosiloff refused to go.

"I feel like prowling around," he said.

That night he came down with fever, and Ivan stayed up all night to apply hot poultices to him and feed him hot water and rum. The next day he was raving about his castle in Siberia and about the fortune he would amass as soon as he outfitted his own boat. Metek stood beside Ivan looking down at the master.

"He is in a bad way," Ivan said.

"He talks much," Metek agreed.

"Go to the galley and have Vatchel make hot broth," Ivan ordered.

Metek slipped away and went to the galley. Vatchel shook his head when Metek gave Ivan's order.

"The man's sins have caught up with him," he said. "I would rather be the cook than the man who beat and made slaves out of other men that he might make money."

"He needs the hot soup," Metek reminded Vatchel.

"It will do him no good, but I will make it." The cook rattled a pot and slammed it on the stove. "Last night I had a dream in which we buried a bearded man as big as the master. My dreams are always signs of what will happen." He tossed bits of meat into the pot and poured water over them. "Before you cured me of scurvy I dreamed I was eating a raw steak cut from a deer."

"Is that why you ate the raw meat?" Metek asked.

He, too, believed in dreams. Kablunth always foretold coming events by dreams.

"That is why I ate and was cured," Vatchel said.

Metek nodded and said, "So the bearded one will die."

Vatchel turned around quickly. "No, I did not say that. It is very unlucky to say a thing like that." He shook a wooden spoon at Metek. "But you may be right."

Metek carried the steaming broth to the cabin and Ivan held the master's shaggy head up while he forced a few spoons of the steaming liquid between his teeth. Kosiloff ate little of the broth but he did regain his mind for a matter of several hours. He lay staring at Ivan for a long time, then spoke in a weak voice.

"While I live you are not to abandon the ship or her cargo—that is an order."

Ivan nodded grimly. "We will stay with the ship."

Kosiloff closed his eyes and lay still. Ivan remained beside him while he slept. Finally Vatchel and Metek came in. The cook waddled across the planking.

"You had best get some sleep. I will stay here while you sleep. The boy will keep an eye on the men and waken you if need be." Vatchel dropped down on a stool beside the master's bunk.

"Why should the boy keep an eye on the crew?" Ivan asked.

"Some of the men heard the boy say that he had seen land. There is quiet talk among them of abandoning the ship. They say she will be smashed and sink when the ice breaks, that now is the time to cross to the mainland, while there is a path of ice."

"They will all perish in the first gale that blows up if they try it," Ivan said, shortly.

"Before you do anything about it you should get some sleep," Vatchel urged.

"I will sleep five hours, then I am to be awakened. If there is any sign of trouble before that time, you are to waken me." He got to his feet wearily and turned toward the deck.

Metek followed him out to the men's shelter and seated himself against the wall where he pretended to go to sleep. The Cossacks were accustomed to seeing the Innuit boy sleep any place he lay or sat, so they paid no attention to him. They gathered around the carpenter and talked in low, guttural voices.

"You, Stoorman, have you made sleds?" one of the men asked.

The carpenter grunted assent. "I have three sleds such as *they* use in hunting. We will take that one and have four. On four sleds we can haul supplies enough to carry us across the ice."

"We will need guns and powder and ball," another said.

"You trust me as leader?" Stoorman asked.

The men all agreed. One of them said, "We trust you and will do as you say if what you say is what we want."

Stoorman glared at the speaker. "I would as soon run you through with my knife, here and now, Veit. Let me hear no more out of your big mouth."

The others frowned at Veit and he scowled back at them. Through half-closed eyes, Metek watched. They reminded him of a pack of huskies. Stoorman was the strongest and the meanest, so he was the king-dog. Like Karsuk, he would rule, because no man dared stand against him.

"Now," Stoorman said. "Three of you will steal guns from the cabin when the fat one falls asleep, which he will very soon. Get ten guns, that will be enough to carry." He looked about the circle of faces and went on. "Two of you"—he nodded to a pair of Cossacks seated in front of him—"take care of Ivan before he wakens. Lash him to his bunk and gag his big mouth. I will take care of the cook. We'll have no need for him."

"How about the savage?" Veit asked. "He may have been listening to what we have said."

"No ear could hear what we said across that distance," Stoorman answered. "We will take the savage along as hunter and guide."

"Kosiloff would want to stay with his precious furs," one of the men said, and laughed harshly.

"He will stay, neatly tied to his bunk, as will the fat cook and Ivan. We'll have no more of their talk," Stoorman promised.

Metek's sharp ears were far better than Stoorman thought. He had heard every word, but he dared not move until the men had broken up their conference. To do so would have let them know he had been listening. He sat with his eyes closed, snoring loudly.

"Now is as good a time as any," Stoorman said as he rose to his feet.

The men got up and moved away, some below decks, others outside the shelter. Metek knew they would make all their preparations before attacking Ivan and Vatchel. He turned over and scurried across the deck. As he disappeared down the companionway leading to Ivan's cramped little room he heard a rough voice shout, "Where you going. Come back here!"

He did not stop, but rushed to the bunk and shook the mate. Ivan sat up, wide awake at once.

"What's up?" he asked as his boots hit the deck.

"The men will steal the guns and then bind you and Vatchel. They will run away across the ice," Metek explained, his words tumbling out, a mixture of Russian and Innuit.

Ivan leaped to the corner where his and Metek's muskets stood.

"Take your gun. Come with me," he snapped.

They started out upon the deck. Metek was close behind Ivan and when the mate halted, Metek bumped into him. He looked past Ivan's thick form and saw three Cossacks coming out of the master's cabin with guns.

"Drop those!" Ivan barked as his musket came up.

The men did not drop the guns. They jumped back into the cabin and a minute later three muzzles poked past the paneling.

"You'd best let us go as we want," one of the Cossacks called. "We'll blast you if you try to stop us. We're through with being cattle for Kosiloff."

"You fools, you'll freeze to death if you try a crossing," Ivan parried.

At that moment Stoorman appeared above. He took in the situation at once and realized his plans had miscarried. He bellowed down to the three men.

"Pass guns out from the opening on the port side." Then he leaped away to order other men to get the guns.

Ivan knew he could not stop the men from passing the guns out. He was neatly trapped. The men could not get to him without being fired upon but neither could he hope to charge out and cover them. The three men at Kosiloff's door stopped that.

"Keep back and get ready to shoot," Ivan said to Metek as he crouched down beside the door.

None of the Cossacks showed themselves but Metek and Ivan could hear Stoorman giving orders. Boxes rattled and supplies were dragged across the deck. A quarrel broke out when one of the men located Kosiloff's last bottle of rum.

After a time, the men went over the side and Ivan moved carefully out of his berth. The Cossacks were shouting and talking below upon the ice. Ivan ran to Kosiloff's cabin, with Metek at his heels.

They found Vatchel lying on the floor trussed and gagged. Ivan slashed the cook's bonds and Vatchel sat up, spitting and mumbling. Ivan turned to Kosiloff and found that the men had not touched the sick master. Ivan bent over him, then straightened.

"You went to sleep," he said to Vatchel.

"No, but I sat with my back to the door, worse luck," Vatchel grunted. "I'd have given half my pay to have got a grip on the neck of one of those dirty dogs."

Metek stood silently. He was looking toward Kosiloff's bunk. Ivan spoke slowly.

"Go see what they're doing. They might decide to come back."

Metek ran out to the deck and peered through the canvas curtains that served as a door to the deck shelter. The Cossacks were moving across the ice dragging four loaded sleds. They were headed east and south. He turned back to the comparative warmth of the deck room.

Vatchel came out of Kosiloff's cabin moving with unusual speed for a fat man.

"Lend me a hand if they're gone," he called.

Metek went with him to the galley where the cook built up the fire by adding oil to the rocks and sand in the fire box. In a few minutes a kettle of water was boiling.

"Take this to Ivan," Vatchel said. "I'll get some food ready, if those villains left any."

Metek found Ivan working over Kosiloff. The mate applied hot cloth bandages to the master's chest. He rubbed the sick man's arms and shoulders steadily. Kosiloff groaned but showed no other signs of life.

That night Vatchel and Ivan took turns bathing Kosiloff while Metek kept watch in case the Cossacks decided to return to the ship. He listened for the rising of the wind which would be the cause of their turning back, but no gales swept over the ice fields.

Nor did the wind come the next day or the next night. On the third day a terrible storm blew up and raged around the ship for fifteen hours. Metek shook his head when Ivan asked him if he thought the men could have reached the mainland.

"No. They will be out on the rough ice along the shore. They will go very slowly through the rough ice."

"They know, now, what fools they have been," Ivan said grimly.

Metek was making ready to set out on a hunt as soon as the wind died down completely. Vatchel had been able to find only one cask of salted meat. The Cossacks had loaded the rest upon the sleds and had left the one cask only because they had missed it.

"They must have been poking about and found that we had only a little salt meat left. That helped them to make their decision," Ivan said.

"I think they had been planning this for some time and when they heard Metek say the mainland lay to the east and south they decided to make a run for it," Vatchel remarked.

"Will we stay?" Metek asked.

"We will stay until Kosiloff is able to move. He's beaten the fever and will come around if we can get decent food for him. It may be that he will refuse to abandon the ship, even though the crew has left us," Ivan said thoughtfully.

Metek set off on a hunt, heading along the course followed by the men. He and Ivan had fashioned a pair of runners with braces between them and Metek pulled this after him. The trail of the Cossacks had been blown away by the gale and Metek soon decided he could not be sure he was following their course. He shifted his own directly east and moved on.

Toward morning of that day he came to a mountain of upheaved ice and saw bear tracks. Ninoo was accompanied by a little fox who was trailing him to pick up scraps from the great hunter's feast. Metek took up the trail and followed it through the broken tables of ice.

Six hours later he sighted his quarry and began the slow and careful stalk always followed by his people. For more than an hour he ran and slid on his stomach and crawled. At last he was rewarded. The bear halted and began digging into a pile of loose ice from which the wind had swept the snow.

Metek crawled up so close to the big beast he could almost shove the musket barrel out and touch the shaggy rump of Ninoo. This time his first shot brought the great one down, dead upon the ice. From a hiding place near by the little fox darted away.

Metek took the choice cuts and made a cache of the rest. He loaded his sled and started back. When he was five miles from the ship the wind began to blow and a gale swept in upon him. He faced it for a mile, then gave up and dug in. Ten hours later he emerged from a deep drift, dug out his sled and went on.

Ivan was watching for him when he came into view. He shouted and Metek shouted back, letting Ivan know he had made a kill. The mate helped Metek hoist the meat on deck. Vatchel was ready with his big knife and his meat ax. Ivan had built no fire in the deck room and it was freezing cold. The inside of the walls was covered an inch thick with white and gleaming frost. The meat not needed for immediate cooking and use was left on the men's table where it would remain frozen hard as rock.

Ivan took part of the liver and some frozen blood to Kosiloff while Metek and Vatchel sat in the warm galley and ate a hearty meal from what was left. Ivan came in grinning and joined them.

"He eats the raw meat like a wolf whelp," he said.

After they had eaten some of the raw flesh Vatchel cooked a roast and they sat down to a regular meal. Kosiloff, with his remarkable vitality, was able to eat some of the roast, too.

Metek went with Ivan to the cabin. Kosiloff had changed much since his sickness. He did not growl or complain and he treated Ivan as an equal. He had been angry because the men had deserted, but he kept insisting they would return. Ivan disagreed; he believed the Cossacks had all perished of the cold.

"You saw no traces of them?" Kosiloff asked of Metek. It was the first time he had ever spoken to the boy directly.

"I saw no traces. The wind blew away all of their tracks," Metek answered.

"But they will come back, don't you think?" Kosiloff asked.

"I think not," Metek answered.

"In that case we shall have our hands full handling ship when the ice breaks up," Kosiloff said and smiled.

Ivan laughed. "We will, indeed," was all he said.

18. DAWN

A great mountain of ice rose off the port bow of the *Petr*. Its ragged slabs and spires glittered in the twilight of coming day. Ivan and Metek sat on the topmost ridge and looked toward the east. For days they had been keeping watch. The first red traces of dawn were expected very soon and Metek's eagerness for the return of the wanderer was not greater than Ivan's. The weary months which lay behind them were like the shadowy memory of a nightmare.

Ivan brooded upon the trials ahead of them. The greatest dangers were yet to be met. Kosiloff was determined to stay with his ship and to sail back to Siberia with the fortune he had stored in her hold. If they waited until the ice broke up the ship might be smashed, then they would be out in the ice-filled ocean with only a small boat, open and unprotected. The prospect was not very bright but Ivan had come to share Kosiloff's determination to sail the *Petr* home if possible.

Metek stirred, his face was turned toward his homeland and he was thinking of the village above Point Barrow. The

people would be making ready for a great festival of welcome to the sun. Etah and the hunters would be bringing
in game, the kayaks would be repaired and oiled. Ivan
turned to him and noticed the expression on the boy's
face.

"What are you thinking of?" he asked.

"At home the people will be making ready to welcome
the sun," Metek said.

"And you would be with them?" Ivan asked.

"Yes," Metek replied.

"You would not wish to sail south with us to Petropavlovsk and later to the China ports?"

"I would return to the village of my people," Metek
said. "If I have earned a gun and powder and ball I would
take them with me to show the people that I did not lie
about the white hunters."

Ivan smiled. Metek had told him about leaving the village. Having lived among the Innuits, Ivan knew their ways.
He said nothing about the desperate need they would have
for Metek's help should they be lucky enough to escape
from the ice.

"I will ask Kosiloff to put you ashore when we are free
of the ice," he said.

"That will be good," Metek answered and smiled widely.

The flush of dawn had begun to fade behind the eastern
spire. Another brief glow had vanished and the sun had
not shown his face. They got down from their lookout
and returned to the ship.

The months of captivity since the crew had deserted
them had been months of desperate struggle for food.
Their casks of whale oil had run low and heat had been
scant. They had lived mostly in the galley with Vatchel,
using the fire for heat as well as for cooking. There had
been days of fasting while Metek and Ivan hunted upon

the ice. They had eaten fox and bear, with one seal to vary the fare. The drift of the ice had ceased after their floe had jambed hard against a heavy raft of shore ice. When the masses had met the mountain off the port bow had been formed and they were able to see the shore line far away and dim.

Kosiloff was grim and silent but he treated all of them as his equals after recovering from his illness. They shared, equally, the heat and the food and the cramped sleeping quarters in the galley.

Vatchel began to worry about the return of the sun. He placed little faith in the reckonings of Kosiloff and Ivan. It was possible, he argued, that they had floated clear to the north pole and that the sun would never rise.

"And if the sun does not rise the ice will never break up," he would say; then he would spread his pudgy hands and groan.

But the sun did come. The light increased until there was broad daylight at noon. Vatchel became happy again. He had a very accurate method of checking upon the increase in daylight. From his sea bag he dug a small prayer book. Every day at noon he would slide down the ice steps and run out toward the cliffs, book in hand, trying to read by the returning light. When he was able to make out the finest print he was satisfied that the wanderer was really going to return.

The ice began to boom and crack and the *Petr* shuddered many times as the movement wrenched her timbers. Metek kept a close watch for open water and finally located a lane between the ship and the shoreline. As the lane opened, the walrus came, as though by magic. Their bellowing could be heard when the wind was right. Ivan and Metek staged a hunt and killed a small animal. No longer was there a problem of getting food, but Kosiloff's orders that the casks be filled with salted meat kept the two hunters busy every day.

They were out on the ice stalking walrus when the sun appeared. Metek had driven his harpoon into a young bull that Ivan had wounded. Both were toiling upon the rope when the sun thrust his face above the mass of round hills to the east, bathing the sea in purple light, glistening upon the icy spires.

"Look! There upon the ice foot!" Metek shouted and almost let go the harpoon line.

"The sun!" Ivan straightened his bent back.

The walrus, making a last desperate plunge, hit the line hard. Metek and Ivan went down and had to scramble and dig to keep from being hauled into the icy water and down to their deaths. They battled grimly and the walrus, which was near dead from Ivan's shot, came up slowly and made one last rush at the edge of the ice. The two hunters scrambled back and got themselves set. When they finally anchored the carcass and looked toward the east the sun was gone.

"Anyway, we saw him," Ivan said as he wiped spray from his face.

"We did," Metek agreed.

After that the sun appeared daily, but with his coming he brought wind and bitter cold. It seemed unreasonable that the coldest weather should be after the coming of the sun, but for weeks the temperature hovered near fifty below and the open lanes of water would have frozen over again but for the gales.

The wind made hunting impossible except on one or two days each week. Metek and Ivan brought in the walrus and Kosiloff and Vatchel cut up the meat and packed it away. Blubber was stacked for fuel and fresh meat was eaten daily. None aboard the *Petr* now had any scruples against eating a portion of it raw. They all openly admitted that frozen walrus blubber and steak was as fine a dish as any cooked food. They were strong and healthy, eager for the test which was to come.

The sea opened and the ice tumbled about as the gales whipped the water to foam. In her little ice harbor under the lee of the ice mountain the *Petr* remained frozen tight. From the high ridge above the ship, Ivan and Metek watched the arrival of the first birds. A raven came wheeling down wind and perched himself upon a pinnacle above the ship. He cocked his black head first on one side and then on the other. His hard, round eyes glittered as he croaked a dismal welcome before flying off toward the mainland. Little snow buntings swept around the cliffs or alighted upon the rigging of the ship, then whirled away. A burgomaster gull wheeled overhead on the third day after they had seen the raven. His flight was northward, as though he had caught the sound of tumbling seas, and he was leading his mate, who came sailing after him, to a nuptial retreat on some bleak, wave-beaten island.

Impatiently the men waited. Metek was worried because the opening lanes cut off their pathway to the land. He was somewhat assured when Ivan told him that they could always take to one of the small boats, rowing it across the open water and dragging it across any ice rafts that might block their path. Vatchel was in high spirits, certain that nothing could prevent their escape. He had had a dream in which he saw himself dining with old friends at the inn in Petropavlovsk. Kosiloff was silent and watchful, keeping a close eye upon the ice near the ship and upon the ship itself.

The casks were well filled with meat and there was little to do except to tear away the deck shelter and make what repairs they could upon the sails and the rigging.

One morning Metek discovered a crack in the ice near
the ship. He ran to tell Ivan and they went on deck together. Kosiloff was called and Vatchel came with him.
They stood at the rail in silence. A heavy swell had set into
the harbor from the southwest. A strong southerly wind
outside was working upon the ice. As the men watched, the
crack widened and others opened.

"If this lasts for twelve hours we will be freed," Ivan
observed.

The crashing of the ice smothered Kosiloff's reply. It
filled the air with grinding and booming. Metek clung to
the rail and stared at the sea. He was not greatly worried,
because he was certain even the terror of breaking ice could
not harm this big ship. Vatchel pulled at his double chin
with nervous fingers and muttered. For the first time since
the coming of the sun, he was worried. The sea presented
such a wild and terrible spectacle that he finally shuffled
back to the galley and sat down.

The seas continued to roll in during the day and more
cracks opened across the icy harbor, until the swell at last
reached the *Petr*. Late in the afternoon a split in the ice
came directly amidships of the vessel. This was the danger
both Ivan and Kosiloff feared. The ice quickly loosened
around the bows, but held around the stern. The wrenches
given the *Petr* by the first movements made every timber
in her creak and groan.

"What would you say we should do?" Kosiloff asked.

"There is nothing to do but wait. If she is wrenched
apart we will have time to launch a boat, but we must have
supplies ready." Ivan turned to Metek. "Come," he said.

They hurried to the galley to get Vatchel's help. The
cook heaved himself to his feet, and began dragging his sea
bag toward the deck when Ivan told him they must get
supplies on deck.

"So, we are to abandon ship!" he shouted.

Ivan kicked the bag aside. "If we do you can't take that bag in a small boat."

"But I have my silk shirt and my pantaloons for dress-up in that bag," Vatchel argued. "I do not leave such things to be sunk with this ship."

"You do leave them," Ivan snapped. "But we are not sinking, and we may not sink. We are making ready in case we do have to abandon ship."

Vatchel grunted and set to work helping get the supplies on deck and piled beside the rail. When the work was finished Ivan and Metek joined the master at the rail.

The *Petr* had worked her way forward a bit. She gave a lurch to port, which loosened the ice from under her counter, and she was afloat, though grinding uncomfortably. Ivan and Kosiloff were elated to feel again the motion of the sea under their feet.

The *Petr* floated idly, being unable to make any progress because she was hemmed in on all sides by ice, having only a small pool to bathe her sides. The starboard half of her old cradle remained and the men hauled her to it and made her fast with ice anchors.

The next day was clear and bright and a light wind was blowing. Ivan, Kosiloff and Metek were keeping a vigilant watch at the rail while Vatchel sat in the galley like an ostrich hiding its head from danger. All eyes were fixed upon the ice on the port side, some twenty-five yards distant, which had commenced to move toward the *Petr*. They were fascinated by the danger of the approaching monster.

The ice moved slowly, steadily up to the *Petr's* port side. Foot by foot, the open water vanished as the great cakes moved forward. They touched the sides of the ship, gently at first, then with a force that made her shudder. Slowly

she heeled over four degrees, eight, then twelve to starboard with her port bilges heavily pressed.

For two hours the *Petr* lay straining in the viselike grip.
At times the pressure lessened and she would almost right
herself, then again she would heave over until she listed
above twenty degrees. On the starboard side, while she was
heeling, the nip was felt on her timberheads, which were
the weakest parts of her frame, but on the port side she
was pressed below the turn of the bilge. Her fate depended
upon whether she could lift when the final thrust of the
nip came.

The hour which decided her fate came sooner than Ivan
had expected. There was a movement of the ice and the
timbers of the *Petr* fairly cracked and screamed, then she
heaved upward, righted herself and sat balanced clear of the
water. There she rode for a few minutes. The ice ground
and crunched under her like the teeth of a monster that
had sought to crush and swallow her. It seemed the ice had
decided it could not clamp her in its maw, and would,
therefore, release her. It slipped away slowly and the *Petr*
sank down with a lurch that sent Metek sprawling across
the deck. Ivan and Kosiloff braced themselves and clung to
the rail.

"She's free!" Ivan shouted.

Metek scrambled to his feet and swayed to the rail. The
Petr was floating in a narrow lane of water. The lane
widened until there was a wide waterway leading out to the
open sea beyond the ice field where the ship had rested for
many months. Kosiloff sprang into action.

"Get some canvas on her!" he shouted.

Vatchel was called and the four men labored to make
what sail they could. The Petr responded and slid down the
lane, nosing through the broken ice toward the rolling,
raft-filled waters beyond. She slid out of her prison and

plowed proudly into the waves beyond the floe.

"Like I said!" Vatchel shouted as he danced up and down, his fat paunch bobbing, his long hair flying in the wind.

Kosiloff smiled at the cook. "The sea has been good to us," he said.

"You have been rewarded for courage, sir," Ivan said. He was willing to admit that Kosiloff's unwavering determination to bring his ship through had saved them.

"This is the job of men who do not turn from their duty. I have learned much from it," Kosiloff said, and smiled.

Metek stood watching his friends. He only vaguely understood, but he was aware that the master had changed much since he had first seen him. Vatchel was sent to the galley to prepare a hot meal while Kosiloff and his two-man crew worked ship.

19. RELEASED

The *Petr* glided gently out into the sea. Metek watched the mountain of ice, which had afforded shelter from the gales through the long winter, as it dropped astern. The piled slabs of ice were breaking up, splitting apart and plunging into the sea. Even Metek realized that they had escaped none too soon. The wind died and Ivan made the ship fast to a friendly berg that floated low in the water.

That night Metek sat on the deck and watcned the stars twinkle feebly through the twilight. Now that the sun had returned there was never any deep darkness. The rolling hills loomed close by and he had a powerful desire to put his feet upon them, to run and shout, and to start up the coast toward his home.

Vatchel came out and sat beside him. The cook had talked with Ivan and had learned that Metek desired to

188

leave the ship and return to his home. Vatchel was sure Kosiloff would never listen to this, because Metek would be needed to help sail the ship. He had decided to make things easier for the boy by talking to him.

"I'll be shoving my big feet under a table at the Little Horse Inn," he began. "Big Anna will come in from the stoop and I'll say to her, 'Woman, get on some real food.' Big Anna will come in with a platter so big."—Vatchel spread his hands wide—"Son, you should see that platter of Big Anna's. A haunch of deer swimming in brown gravy, a half a baked fish, groat soup, fresh rye bread and a pail of quas to wash it down." Vatchel rubbed his stomach eagerly.

"I would like to see Big Anna's platter," Metek said eagerly. Vatchel had cleverly touched upon one thing any Innuit is always interested in—food.

"I'd take you to the Little Horse, son. We'd climb up the hill to Father Alec's and he'd make a good Christian out of you. Big Anna never lets no heathens set their feet down under her tables, nor any infidels or Anabaptists, but, with Father Alec's grace to go with you, you'd be welcome as me." Vatchel leaned forward, watching Metek's face.

Metek beamed. "I would like that," he said.

"And we'd see a lot of things that'd make your eyes pop, son, like the cannon down at the port, them big guns that watch the harbor, and the shops with everything laid out to look at." Vatchel chuckled. "You'd have your pay from Kosiloff and be as rich as me, I'll bet on that, because I've been watching the master. He's a changed man and I wager an honest one now."

"I could get presents to take to my village," Metek said, and laughed.

"Presents!" Vatchel laid special force upon his words. "You could get the most beautiful things, a shipload of them." He leaned over and tapped Metek upon the knee and winked slyly. "But there's something else that will please you."

Metek listened eagerly, wondering what could be better than the food and the presents Vatchel had spoken about.

"There will be many beautiful girls," Vatchel explained. "All through this spring sunshine they will cover their faces with the intestine of the bear stuck on with fresh lime, and by the time we reach Petropavlovsk they will have taken it off and have painted their cheeks with fat and seaweed. Those girls will be red-cheeked and plump and they'll laugh and sing for us."

Unknowingly, Vatchel had spoiled his whole story. Metek was not thinking of the beautiful Kamchatka girls, he was thinking of Lito and the times they had spent on the beach and on the slopes above Eiber village. A sudden wave of homesickness swept over him. Lito running along the shore with the waves licking at her flying, brown feet, her hair blowing around her oval face, her laugh ringing out as she sped away from him. He said nothing and Vatchel glanced at him sharply, realizing too late that he had touched a very tender spot.

"You left a girl, prettier perhaps than those at Petropavlovsk?" he asked softly.

"Yes," Metek answered sadly. "I think Masumah has taken her back to my father's village to be his wife."

Vatchel, ever the romancer, in spite of his fat bulk, at once forgot that he was supposed to make Metek want to sail south. He spoke softly. "Perhaps she will wait for you, son," he said.

"I do not know, but how can I know until I return? Her father looked with much favor upon Masumah and *he* looked all eyes upon Lito." Metek twisted a bit of thong around his fingers until it cut deep into the flesh of his hand.

"But you asked her to wait for you?" Vatchel persisted.

"I said I would come back," Metek answered.

Vatchel suddenly remembered what he was supposed to do. He began talking all at once.

"From that port we will go on with the ship to the China ports and there you will see such things as I cannot describe, such tall ships as will make the *Petr* look like a little boat, sloops of war from many countries, traders of the Britons who sail into every port on earth, the merchantmen for Spain, with sloops of war mounted with brass cannon lying alongside to see them safely back to their home ports. You can buy a sea chest full of sparkling jewels for your friends up here and cloth of every color." Vatchel hurried along, expanding the picture, but he saw that Metek was not listening; he was looking across the icy waters to where the round hills loomed in the moonlight.

While they talked, Ivan was speaking with Kosiloff in the master's cabin. His talk had to do with Metek's future, too.

"The boy would leave us and travel to his home," he said.

Kosiloff considered this for some moments, then he looked up at Ivan. "My first duty is to take the *Petr* safely to port and turn her over to the merchants who built her and fitted her out for me. Without the boy we cannot sail her out of this ocean with its ice and its adverse winds. I would have him go home, but I cannot do as I wish."

"He had no small part in saving the ship," Ivan said.

"I grant his part and he shall share in the returns we receive," Kosiloff said. "He shall receive an equal part." He looked steadily at his mate. "I believe now, though I once did not think that way, that we will make a safe return."

"He will never return to his home," Ivan went on, determined to lay his case before Kosiloff. "No ship will

ever again venture into this desolation and danger. He will
be an exile in a strange land."

"Ships will come into the sea; they will sail it from the
pole to its eastward limits. It may well be that they will
sail by a northeast passage to Britain and France and Spain.
It may be many years, but men never let a sea alone once
they have found it. That there is nothing here but ice and
dead shores will not stop them. If Russia does not claim
this land the British or the Spanish will. No, I must take the
boy with me and you must make a sailor out of him. It is
the only way."

Ivan nodded. He had known Metek must go, but he felt
that he must speak for the young Innuit. Now that he had
spoken he would say no more.

"Good night, sir," he said, as he got to his feet.

"Good night," Kosiloff answered.

Ivan went out on the deck. He saw the dark forms of
Vatchel and Metek, but he did not go near them. The cook
was following his orders, talking to the boy. It might be
that Vatchel would win Metek over. He retired to his bunk.

The next day the *Petr* moved on, sailing south at a fair
pace with favorable winds to send her heeling down the
coast. The clumsy navigation possible with her limited crew
served very well as long as the winds were favorable and no
spring gale struck them.

Metek watched as he worked beside Ivan. He watched
their course, knowing the ship was carrying him away from
his home. At last Ivan spoke to him.

"I would have put you ashore, but we cannot sail the
ship without you, Metek. I spoke to the master and he
rightly said that his first duty was to take the *Petr* safely to
port."

Metek nodded, his face expressionless. "Yes," he said.

"If ever a ship sails north into this ocean I will see that
you are aboard her," Ivan promised.

"Yes," Metek said, and his eyes remained upon the low-lying shore, seeking some landmark that would tell him where they were.

"Perhaps you will forget the north when you see the wonders of the world," Ivan said. He felt he must say something, because the quiet manner of the boy worried him.

"Perhaps," Metek agreed.

Vatchel bellowed from the galley. "Soup! Men! Soup!"

Kosiloff made his way down from the rigging where he had been scanning the coast ahead. Ivan stayed at the helm while Kosiloff and Metek ate with Vatchel. Then Kosiloff took the helm and Ivan ate his meal.

That night the *Petr* sailed southward, feeling her way through loose rafts of ice, scudding across the open water, making good time as she fled out of the desolation which had held her captive so many months. Metek stayed on deck a long time, keeping watch at the helm with Ivan, who set a safe course well away from the coast. His plan was simple, he would follow the shore line until they came to the Aleutian chain and from there they could sail across the narrow sea to the coast of Siberia.

In the morning Metek stood at the rail scanning the coast line. The rolling hills seemed familiar but he could not remember any landmark. He had no idea how far into the northern ocean the *Petr* had been carried by the drifting ice. Now it was late spring, and he had traversed much of the coast in the winter and during the time of darkness. Suddenly he bent forward, his eyes fixed upon the shore.

A ridge came down to the sea topped by rocky bluffs. Beyond the ridge a spiral of wood-smoke lifted against the sky. Metek leaped forward and halted beside Ivan, who was at the helm. He pointed toward the spiral of smoke.

"A fire," he almost shouted.

Ivan looked and nodded his head, but he made no movement to swing the ship shoreward. Metek leaned over the
rail and watched as the mouth of a river swung slowly into
view.

"It is Eiber—Eiber village!" he shouted.

"Is it your home village?" Ivan asked.

"No, but I lived there during the winter." Metek faced
the helmsman. "If we could stop for just an hour."

Ivan smiled. Vatchel had told him about the talk he had
had with Metek.

"She lives here?" Ivan asked softly.

"Unless she has gone with Masumah. I would know before I go on." Metek spoke slowly, but his eyes were eager.

"We will heave to and stop an hour or so," Ivan said. He
swung the *Petr* over and she slid toward the mouth of the
river.

"Why are we shifting inshore?" Kosiloff's voice boomed
from the stern. He came forward, a frown on his face.

"This is the village where Metek lived one winter," Ivan
explained. "He would stop an hour or so."

Kosiloff looked at Metek a long minute, then slowly
nodded his head. "I know you will come back to the *Petr*
after you have seen your friends," he said.

"I will come," Metek promised. He could scarcely con-
tain himself, he was so eager.

Kosiloff, Vatchel and Metek worked ship as she slid
slowly into the deep channel of the river. Ivan laid her over
along a wall of rock and she felt her way until she was close
inshore. The anchor dropped and she lay lifting and
dropping.

Metek could see the summer village on the beach with
men and women swarming down to the shore. Never had
they seen such a ship and they came slowly, half afraid to
approach. A hundred yards from the water they halted and
stood staring at the great kayak.

Eagerly Metek's eyes ran along the line of men and women. He recognized Noosha and Lito's mother and several others, but he saw nothing of the girl. He was surprised at the number of people gathered at Eiber village. Several other villages must have moved in to join Noosha and his people.

Ivan and Metek lowered a boat and set off toward the shore. When they beached the boat, Metek leaped out and shouted to the Innuits who stood well back from the beach, ready to whirl and flee. Noosha and several others recognized the boy and a shout went up. The whole crowd broke and ran down to meet the visitors.

They pushed in around Metek and Ivan. Their wonder at the white-faced hunter was great, and their wonder at Metek was almost as great. He had gone out and found the white-faced hunters and the great ship. He had proved that he had not lied or made up big stories to impress his elders. They chattered and shouted, and were surprised and delighted when Ivan spoke a few words of Innuit to them.

Several times Metek tried to ask about Lito, but he never got the words out of his mouth. Every one of the men was asking questions about the wonders he had seen and about the great ship and about the people he had met. Finally Metek edged back as a circle formed around a cookfire. Ivan saw that Metek was trying to slip away and boldly took charge of the conversation. He talked so loud and so rapidly that every man bent forward, forgetting about Metek.

Metek slipped away to the tent of Noosha. He paused at the entrance and peered inside. One of Lito's little brothers sat on the floor chewing a strip of seal blubber.

"Where is Lito?" Metek asked.

The little boy looked up and fright made his eyes very round. "She does not live here any more." Before Metek could say another word the boy ducked under the flap of

the tent and ran as fast as he could toward the circle of
Innuits seated around the cook-fire.

Metek turned down toward the beach. He walked slowly,
looking up at the bluffs where he and Lito had caught little
auks. The sea swallows were diving and dipping over the
rocky slope in countless thousands. Then he looked down
toward the sea with its stretch of sandy beach leading away
to where the bluffs came down to dip their rocky feet in
the booming surf. Slowly Metek walked along the beach.
He did not want to go back to the people. Noosha would
tell him how Lito had gone with Masumah to the village at
Point Barrow. He did not want to be told about it.

Suddenly he heard a shout and lifted his face so that the
cold wind blew against it. There, running toward him from
the rocky bluff, came Lito, her hair flying in the wind, her
little feet flashing over the sand.

"Metek! Metek!" she cried as she raced toward him.

Metek stood with arms open wide, his voice stuck tight
in his throat. Lito fairly leaped into his arms, and he tipped
back her head to look at her face.

"I said you would come. I made a house for us and I
moved into it. I have kept that house for you." Her words
tumbled out eagerly, wildly.

"Lito, you are beautiful," Metek said, using the Russian
word Vatchel had taught him.

"Beautiful?" Lito looked puzzled.

Metek laughed, "I will teach you many very fine words,"
he said. "That one means I saw no woman like you in all
my travels."

Lito looked out at the *Petr.* "You came in that great
boat?"

"Yes," Metek said and his face grew sober.

Instantly Lito gripped his arms hard. "You are not

leaving in that great boat?" There was sudden fear in her eyes.

"Yes, Lito. I have promised. But I will come back as soon as I have helped sail her home. I will come with many presents for you."

"I do not want presents," Lito said. "No, you must not go. If you go I shall have to marry Masumah. My father promised him and he will soon come with his kayak for me."

"I will speak to Noosha," Metek said sternly.

They walked up to the circle of people around the cookfires. Everyone laughed when they halted arm in arm. Ivan looked and his eyes held an odd glint. He got to his feet and spoke to Metek.

"Fifteen villagers from far to the south are staying here. They wish to sail with us on the *Petr* as far as their village. In that time I could teach a number of them to be sailors, I believe, and some of them seem eager to go on an adventure." He smiled widely. "I think with their help we could get on without you."

Metek's brown hand tightened over Lito's. She did not understand what Ivan had said, but she knew it was good news—she could feel it.

"So you and this pretty one can borrow a kayak and set out for home as soon as you go with me to the ship and get your gun and several things I am sure Kosiloff will want to give you." He turned to Lito. "You will come on board, too. Your father is going to look at the ship."

Metek turned to Lito and began to explain. He mixed his Innuit and his newly learned Russian and his words tumbled over one another but Lito understood everything he said.

20. HOME AGAIN

Metek dipped his paddle deep and sent the kayak darting across the green swell. He had rigged a two-hole boat similar to the bidarkas of the Aleuts. Seated in front of him was Lito. The eyes of both were turned back to where a group of men and women stood upon the beach. Far out to sea a white square of canvas dipped as though sending a farewell signal. Metek's eyes shifted to the sail and he smiled.

"I shall miss the ship and my friends," he said.

"But we have many things. The big man with so much red hair on his face gave me many wonderful presents, and you were given hunting things such as no Innuit has ever had."

"I am eager to reach home," Metek said as he gave his attention to his paddle. "Now the people will believe and it may be that I will be the story-teller and not Kablunth."

The kayak slipped swiftly along the bleak shore. Hour after hour, Metek and his bride-to-be moved farther north along the coast. At last they halted and beached the boat. A camp was made and bird's eggs gathered by Lito, while

Metek proudly demonstrated the power of the white-man's gun by shooting a young caribou that had wandered down to the beach. They made a feast and laughed and sang until they were so sleepy they could not stay awake any longer. Lito rolled up in her robe on one side of the boat and Metek rolled up in his on the other side. They slept long and peacefully.

The next morning as they were making ready to launch their heavily laden boat, they sighted a kayak dancing over the water. Its occupant had seen them and was heading toward the beach. As the kayak drew near they saw the round face of Masumah peering at them.

"He goes to Eiber village for a bride," Lito said and laughed.

"We will greet him," Metek said. He stood up and shouted.

Masumah slid his kayak up on the beach and sat looking at Metek, a black frown upon his face. Finally he spoke. "You had best stay away from my village, and I will now take Lito with me." He began unfastening the thongs which held his jacket to the boat's ring.

"If you go on to Eiber village you will find a bride there," Lito said.

"If you turn back with us you may join our wedding feast," Metek said.

"I suppose you have brought back proof of your stories?" Masumah said, and laughed.

Metek held up the musket so that Masumah could look at it, then he held up a new and shining knife Ivan had given him. Lito lifted a red and yellow jacket from her bed robe, and a string of blue beads that glistened in the sun.

Masumah stared at the strange things, and frowned. Lito was eager to tell him all about Metek's triumph. "If you go on to Eiber village they will tell you about the white-faced hunters and the great ship that is big as a village. They have seen the things Metek talked about."

"I go on, but I will come back, and I will bring a bride," Masumah said. He shoved the kayak into the water and whirled it about without fastening the thongs around his waist.

"There is only the fat girl, Neena, who is not married and she has a terrible tongue, so bad none of the men will have her," Lito said and giggled to herself all the time she was helping Metek load the boat.

They moved on up the coast, driving swiftly, camping when they felt like it, laughing much and making every meal a feast. At last they passed the island and Metek pointed out the cove where he had seen the sunken ship.

"Some day we will go there and see what we can find," he said.

"But now we must hurry on," Lito finished for him.

"Yes, we must hurry, because I must build a warm hut for the coming winter." Metek's paddle boiled the green water as he drove it deep.

The morning sun was shining on the cliffs and Point Barrow was stretching its bony finger toward the north pole when the kayak slid around the promontory and headed in across the last few miles of their journey.

They could see the villagers up on the slope. The summer tents flapped in the wind and smoke swirled down toward the sea from the fire-pits of the women. As they neared the shore, the smell of wood-smoke came to them, and with it the rich and savory odor of roasting caribou meat. For a time none of the villagers noticed the incoming boat. Finally three boys, playing on the beach, saw the kayak and raced, shouting, up the hill.

In true Innuit fashion, the people trooped down to the shore to welcome the visitors. They knew the incoming boatman could not be Masumah, because he had been gone but a few days.

Eagerly Metek watched them as they came down the rocky slope. He saw Kablunth and his father, Etah, and all of the others, every one of them an old friend. As he bent forward, driving the boat toward the landing, he saw that they recognized him and had halted. They were staring at him in silence, but none of them had turned back.

Metek slid the kayak up on the sand and unlaced his belt. Lito quickly freed herself and they stepped out together. They advanced, hand in hand, to the silent group of villagers.

"I have brought proof of all the stories I once told," Metek said.

Then very suddenly he was welcomed, not by the people, but by a yelping dog. Karsuk came charging down out of the village followed by a pack of shaggy huskies and a dozen fat puppies. The big dog leaped up against Metek and tried to lick his face.

"Down, big one," Metek said, and his voice was not very steady.

Etah stepped forward. It was his place to welcome Metek. "You may use my tent," he said, and looked sharply at Lito.

"Father, this is Lito from Eiber village. She has come to you to be my bride." He laughed eagerly, and stepped back to the boat. A moment later he was holding aloft the white-man's musket. "This is the weapon that kills with fire," he said very slowly.

The men crowded around him, leaning forward, staring at the gun, but not touching it. Kablunth finally spoke. "We would see it kill with fire," he said gruffly.

Metek looked around him. On a rock far beyond the range of a lance or a harpoon sat a sea hawk. The king of the air was tearing at a gull he had caught. Carefully Metek examined the musket, then took aim. He pressed the trigger and flames and smoke belched from the gun. The hawk seemed to explode in a swirl of feathers. It fell off the rock dead. Fright showed upon the faces of some of the men; all remained in awed silence.

"You have seen," Metek said.

Then everyone began talking and shouting and trying to pat Metek on the back, but with great care so as not to touch the deadly weapon. The women crowded around Lito and helped her carry her things up to a tent where she would be secluded from Metek until the marriage ceremony.

Like disappearing fog before the sun, the coldness of the men had vanished. Now they were ready to believe any story Metek told. Kablunth walked apart, his face very sour and sad. He knew that he was no longer the story-teller; another had come to take his place.

The men seated themselves around the fire-pits. There was a great abundance of food because the hunting season was good, and much of it was cooking over the fires. The women busied themselves in making the meat ready, leaving a few to sit with Lito. Everyone stuffed himself, but none ate so fast or crammed his mouth so full that he could not ask questions. All were very sad because the great ship had touched at Eiber village and not at Point Barrow, but Metek's description of her was almost as good as seeing her with their own eyes.

And when everyone had eaten all he could eat, and the women had finished their meal, everyone sat back and looked expectantly at Metek. Metek got to his feet. He was now a man and would act as a man should act. He turned toward the tent where Lito was being hidden and strode toward it. His friends watched, their faces wreathed in smiles. Metek did not falter as he approached the tent. At the opening he halted, and called in a loud voice:

"Come out, woman, or I will come in after you."

"You dare not come," Lito called out to him. Her voice sounded very angry, but smothered giggles came from within the tent.

With a swift thrust of his arm Metek tossed aside the sealskin flap and plunged into the tent. A moment later he came out carrying a kicking and fighting Lito, who seemed bent upon scratching his eyes out. The people all shouted loudly, giving Metek very good advice upon the handling of an obstinate woman.

Metek marched through the circle of seated Innuits, straight to a tent which had been vacated by one of Etah's neighbors so that Metek could have a home. He thrust his kicking burden inside the tent and dropped the flap behind them.

Very suddenly Lito ceased kicking, and her arms slid around his neck.

"We are home," she said softly.

"Yes, we are home," Metek said, and held her very close.

Note to the Teacher

No set of questions, discussion topics, appreciation and related activities can be made to fit the needs of all groups equally well. The set given here includes material, some of which is suitable for slow pupils, some for average pupils, and some for gifted pupils, grades 5-8, respectively. The teacher may (a) select from it to suit the needs of a group, or (b) consider it as a guide in working out a comparable set of material, based on *Iceblink* but designed, in its entirety, for use by a specific group.

Before using this material, please read the booklet: *The Group Study of the Novel, Grades 5-8,* written by Jennifer Harvey, B.A., and published by The Book Society of Canada Limited. Note that the teacher's supplementary questions described in this booklet correspond to the questions included here with the text of *Iceblink*. For convenience, the material is arranged under chapters.

It is interesting to note that the author, Rutherford Montgomery, has been a successful writer of books for boys and girls since 1939. He has received high awards for several of his publications. Since 1961, he has done many stories and adaptations for Walt Disney Productions.

QUESTIONS, DISCUSSION TOPICS,
APPRECIATION and RELATED ACTIVITIES

Prepared by
JENNIFER HARVEY, B.A.

1. **FAMINE** (pages 7 to 20)

With almost any novel, certain chapters lend themselves more readily than others to in-depth discussion. The relative importance of the chapters of *Iceblink* for this purpose is indicated by the number and difficulty of the questions. The first chapter, which lays the foundation of the novel, should receive special attention; accordingly, a detailed outline of questioning has been supplied for it. Later chapters may be grouped for assignments according to: (a) their importance, and (b) the age and ability of the group members.

1. **Questions**
    (a) *Vantage Point* (setting)
        (i) In your opinion, what is the main impression the author wishes to convey about the landscape?
        (ii) Is this impression different from what you had expected? Be prepared to explain your answer.

    Vantage Point (time)
        (i) The events described in this novel take place in the 1750s. In this chapter, mention *two* or *three* details that suggest the story is not concerned with modern times.
        (ii) Suggest an important part that time plays in the development of this novel.

    (b) *Character*
        Do you feel sympathetic towards Metek? Do you think you will be able to identify with him in his adventures throughout the novel? Give reasons for your answer.

205

(c) *Conflict*

    (i) What conflict described in this chapter makes you want to read on?

    (ii) What future conflict is suggested? Why does the author give you this hint?

(d) *Point of View*

From what point of view is the story told? Do you consider this an effective way of beginning the novel? Explain why (or why not).

2. **Discussion**

What purposes may the author have had in presenting the habits and customs of the Eskimo in such detail in this chapter?

3. **Appreciation**

(a) Choose *two* appropriate examples, and comment on the author's ability to paint vivid pictures in words.

(b) Locate a *simile* in this chapter, and comment on its effectiveness.

4. **Related Activities**

(a) Art — The group may make a model of the setting, or a mural for classroom display.

(b) Research — (i) On a map, locate exactly the area described in this chapter.

    (ii) In an encyclopaedia, look up facts about the whaling industry of British Columbia in the 1750s.

(c) Film — Show the film* *Angotee* (Story of an Eskimo Boy). NFB 0153021

2. **OUTCAST** (pages 21 to 33)

1. **Questions**

(a) Does the story Metek tells convince you? Give reasons for your answer. If you had been a member of the tribe, do you think you would have believed him?

(b) In your opinion, was the reaction of Metek's parents to his story justified? Give reasons for your answer.

(c) Were you surprised that Karsuk joined Metek on his journey? What was the author's purpose in having the dog do this? Would you agree with Metek's decision

---

*All films mentioned here are obtainable through The National Film Board of Canada.

to keep the dog with him? Give reasons for your answers.

(d) For which participant in the conflict between Metek and the hare (page 32) do you feel the greater sympathy? By what means does the author create sympathy for each participant?

2. **Discussion**

"There is no lance that kills with fire. . ." (page 25). Kablunth, the storyteller, is unwilling to believe Metek's account of the magic lance. What reason does he give for his disbelief? In your opinion, do some people in present-day society try to discourage interest and belief in new developments? For what reasons may they do this? Illustrate by giving examples to substantiate your opinion.

3. **Related Activity** – Show the film *Tuktu and his Eskimo Dogs.* NFB 0166089

^3. **EIBER VILLAGE** (pages 34 to 43)

1. **Questions**

(a) State *two* or *three* aspects of Metek's character that have been revealed more fully in this chapter.

(b) What characteristics, commonly associated with a human, does the little snow-dog appear to possess? What purpose is served by portraying the animal in this way?

(c) On page 38 (middle), the point of view from which the story is narrated changes. From whose point of view is the story now told? Why do you think the author has shifted the point of view at this place?

(d) (i) As a title to this chapter, is "Eiber Village" appropriate, or unappropriate? Give a reason for your answer.

(ii) "The choice of the title, "Eiber Village", is ironic in view of the context." Do you agree with this statement? If so, explain the nature of the irony. If you do not agree that it is ironic, justify your opinion.

2. **Discussion**

"The urge to kill any wild thing he saw was not in Metek. Unlike white men, he killed only for food or for the need of skins and never had a lust to destroy an animal just because he came upon it." (page 38) Discuss, giving reasons for your opinions.

3. **Appreciation**

State *two* or *three* ways in which interest and tension are aroused in the episode of the snow-dog.

4. **Related Activity**

Paying attention to the details given in the text, make a model of the ice plains, hills and mountains described in this chapter.

4. **TOOK-TOO** (pages 44 to 56)

1. **Questions**

(a) Give references from the text to show that the Eskimo is in constant conflict with his surroundings.

(b) Why does Metek keep shouting at the wolves?

2. **Discussion**

(a) Account for the difference in eating habits between Eskimo and white man.

(b) State *two* or *three* ways in which you feel your physical surroundings affect your way of life.

3. **Appreciation**

Find *two* examples each of *metaphor* and *simile* in this chapter. What effects does the author gain by using these figures of speech?

5. **NUTCHOOK** (pages 57 to 63)

1. **Questions**

(a) In this chapter, does Metek's survival depend, to a greater extent, upon his knowledge of the environment and resourcefulness in dealing with its hazards, or upon the instinctive responses of Karsuk to this environment? Support your opinions by reference to the text.

(b) Are you satisfied with the development of the novel up to this point? Give reasons for your answer.

    (c) "In this chapter, a state of hunger is often relieved by the finding of food. By means of this hunger-food pattern, the author (i) furthers our understanding of Eskimo life, and (ii) creates suspense in the outcome of the story." Discuss, using references from the text.

  2. **Appreciation**

    Give *two* or *three* examples of words and phrases that make animals and the elements seem like people. What effect does the author gain by using this device of personification?

  3. **Related Activity**

    Make a graph to indicate the hunger-food pattern frequency. Include your legend, or key, to the graph. (The intensity of the state of hunger might also be plotted.)

6. **THE SUN RETURNS** (pages 64 to 73)

  1. **Questions**

    (a) What character traits do you feel a person should have to be a good hunter?

    (b) Compare the Eskimo methods of hunting land and sea animals.

    (c) (i) Why does Metek think he will be unable to let Karsuk go much farther with him?

       (ii) Do you think Metek's decision to send Karsuk back will be important to the development of the novel? Give reasons for your answer.

    (d) Explain the significance of the discovery of the kayak.

    (e) Why is the return of the sun so important to the Eskimo? What season of the year do you like to see return? Give reasons for your answer.

  2. **Discussion**

    Read carefully the account of the return of the sun (pages 65-67). Is the author trying to give:

    (a) a *scientific explanation* of this physical occurrence;

    (b) a *realistic description* from the point of view of Metek;

    (c) a *symbolic impression* of the sun as the giver of life;

    (d) a combination of (b) and (c)?

    Be prepared to give reasons for your opinion.

  3. **Appreciation**

    (a) On pages 65-67, list details that the author has used to make the scene easy to visualize.

(b) In *either* the paragraph commencing at the bottom of page 68 *or* the second and third paragraphs on page 70, select words which convey both sound and movement. Name *three* ways in which the use of these words serves the author's purpose.

4. **Related Activities**

(a) Research – Find out the reason for the extended period of darkness in the Arctic.

(b) Art – Illustrate pictorially the return of the sun to the Arctic.

(c) Oral Work – Imagine that you are Metek. In a two-minute speech, explain how you might feel if you were in Metek's position (page 73, paragraph 2), and what decision you would make.

7. **THE EIBER VILLAGERS** (pages 74 to 87)

1. **Questions**

(a) In your opinion, was Metek ill-advised not to tell Noosha the real reason he was travelling south? If he had done so at this point, how might the chapter have ended?

(b) Is Metek's decision to leave Eiber Village taken too hastily? Give reasons for your answer.

(c) (i) Up to this point in the novel, which are *principal* and which *secondary* characters? Give reasons for your answer.

(ii) What purpose in the novel do you think the characters, Lito and Masumah, are intended to serve?

(d) Does the ending of this chapter satisfy you? What purpose would have been served by concluding the chapter with Noosha's words "Go and do not come back!"? (See chapter 8, paragraph 6.)

2. **Discussion**

Suppose that the episode of Metek and Lito catching auks had been presented on television rather than through the medium of the printed word. What might have been gained, and what might have been lost, in the televised version?

3. **Related Activity**

Present a television show of the episode above. (Use pictures on a strip of paper which is moved through a shoebox type of screen.) Select the pictures carefully, and write narrative captions as the "voice over" from the announcer.

8. **LONESOME SHORES** (pages 88 to 98)

1. **Questions.**

    (a) Use your atlas to trace Metek's journey up to this point.

    (b) (i) Why does Metek ignore warnings against venturing farther south?

    (ii) What does this indicate about his character?

    (c) State *two* or *three* ways in which the life of the Innuits has been influenced by their geographical environment.

    (d) Give *two* or *three* examples to show how your geographical environment has influenced your way of life.

    (e) (i) What is the purpose of the Eskimo festival "drowning little bladders in the sea"?

    (ii) What do you find most interesting about the ceremony that accompanies this festival?

2. **Discussion**

Select *two* North American festivals celebrated south of the Arctic and compare them with the festival of the "drowning little bladders in the sea", under the following heads:

    (a) why and how originated;

    (b) nature of the ceremonies;

    (c) effect upon the people who participate.

(Note: This discussion topic will require some research.)

3. **Related Activities**

    (a) Research — Read about Indian ceremonial customs of the Kwakuitl and Nootka Indians of British Columbia. The following books will prove useful:

    Indians of the Northwest Coast. Philip Drucker. Natural History Press. N.Y.

    The Whale People. Roderick Haig-Brown. Wm. Collins & Co. Canada Ltd.

(b) Creative Writing — Imagine that Metek attends a Canadian festival south of the Arctic. Write a description of the scene from Metek's point of view.

(c) Film — Show the film *Attiuk*. NFB 0163020

9. **THE SEA-HUNTERS** (pages 99 to 106)

1. **Questions**

(a) At Nushugak, what wonders will be likely to impress Metek most? Give reasons for your answer.

(b) Has the author succeeded in holding your interest throughout his account of Metek's long sea voyage? Explain why (or why not).

(c) (i) Using an atlas, trace the continuation of Metek's journey.

(ii) Is it important for the reader to have an accurate knowledge of Metek's route? Give reasons for your answer.

2. **Discussion**

"The ending of this chapter makes you want to read on." Discuss this statement, and consider the possibilities for the development of the novel in subsequent chapters.

3. **Related Activities**

(a) By means of a pictorial guide (one in which you use appropriate symbols to illustrate events), sum up the story to the end of chapter 9.

(b) (i) Write chapter 10 yourself.

(ii) Read your version to the group for evaluation.

(iii) After you have read the author's chapter 10, compare your account with his.

(iv) Be prepared to compare (with the group) your ability to portray character, develop plot and maintain the reader's interest with that of the author.

10. **THE WHITE MEN** (pages 107 to 115)

1. **Questions**

(a) List *three* details in this chapter that are appropriate for the 1750s.

(b) Contrast the characteristics of Cossack and Aleut as revealed in this chapter.

(c) (i) What traits of character does each of the following appear to possess: Kosiloff, Ivan?

    (ii) How important a role do you think each of these men will play in the novel? Give reasons for your opinion.

2. **Related Activities**

(a) Dramatization – In pairs (or in groups) write and act (or tape-record) a short play dealing with the confrontation of Russians and Aleuts. Try to portray:

(i) tension, and (ii) the lack of a common language.

(b) Creative Writing – In monologue form, write, or be prepared to describe orally, the background story of Ivan's scar.

11. **AMIKUK** (pages 116 to 124)

1. **Questions**

(a) At the beginning of this chapter, the author changes the point of view from which he writes.

    (i) State the point of view from which he is now writing.

    (ii) Do you tend to sympathize and identify with the new point of view presented? Give reasons for your answer.

    (iii) List *two* or *three* details that are particularly effective in arousing sympathy for Amikuk, the sea otter.

(b) "Into this paradise came Kosiloff and his Cossacks." Comment on how this statement succeeds in changing the mood created by the author up to this point in the chapter.

(c) What is the predominant characteristic of Kosiloff? Give examples to support your opinion.

(d) In what respects can the Cossacks' actions and behaviour be (i) condemned, (ii) condoned?

(e) Do you think that the Aleuts of this novel will rebel? Be prepared to support your opinion by references to the text.

2. **Discussion**
   (a) "Revolution has its roots in oppression." Citing examples from history (French, Russian, American revolutions) and from present-day situations, support or refute this statement.
   (b) "In the eighteenth century, the slaughter of the otter off the British Columbia coast was no crueller than the present-day slaughter of the seal in the gulf of St. Lawrence." Discuss.
   (c) "Commercial exploitation frequently follows exploration." Discuss.

3. **Related Activity**
   Research — If suitable books and materials are available, pairs of students might be asked to compare the Cossack behaviour towards the primitive Aleut with that of European explorers towards the natives of North America, South Africa, Australia or New Zealand.

12. **WHALE HUNT** (pages 125 to 129)
    1. **Questions**
       (a) What is meant by (i) magic, (ii) superstition?
       (b) Show, by reference to the text, how an Aleut whale hunt involves both magic and superstition.
       (c) Explain why the identification of the spear point is left until the end of the feast.
       (d) Explain, by reference to the text, whether Kagia is given any specific personality traits, or is depicted as a "typical" Aleut.

    2. **Appreciation**
       (a) Make a list of words and phrases which the author uses to convey the size of the whale.
       (b) Which of these do you feel is the most effective, and why?

13. **THE WHITE-MAN'S SHIP** (pages 130 to 136)
    1. **Questions**
       (a) The author has set up a number of conflicts in this novel: man versus environment; man (Metek) versus man (people of his village); Russians versus Aleuts;

Kosiloff versus Cossacks; Kosiloff versus Ivan. Which of these conflicts do you feel will become the most important in the development of the novel? Give reasons for your opinion.

(b) Has your original conception of Kosiloff's character (see chapter 10) been strengthened or weakened by his portrayal in this chapter? Explain your answer.

(c) From this chapter, identify *six* characteristics of Kosiloff's personality. Which of these is most useful to him in his present position? Which are likely to prove his downfall? Give reasons for your answer.

14. **PRISONER** (pages 137 to 146)

1. **Questions**

(a) In what way do the events of this chapter further the plot of the novel?

(b) How does the author make sure that Vatchel will quickly gain the reader's attention and sympathy?

(c) (i) Explain the element of chance that assures Vatchel's friendship for Metek.

(ii) Is this friendship likely to prove important to each? Give reasons for your answer.

2. **Appreciation**

(a) Choose and evaluate any passage you feel is particularly effective in suggesting the fury of the storm. (Note the author's appeal to the sense of colour and sound.)

(b) Find *five* examples of comparisons made by Metek and Vatchel. (Example: Vatchel compares Kosiloff to a "varmint-skinning pirate", page 145.)

(c) Explain the effectiveness of each comparison you chose in (a) above.

15. **ICEBLINK** (pages 147 to 155)

1. **Questions**

(a) Find *three* references in this chapter to the title of the novel.

(i) To what does the title *Iceblink* refer, and of what significance is the word in this chapter?

(ii) Do you consider it an appropriate title for the novel? Be prepared to justify your answer.

(b) (i) By what means does the author succeed in making realistic the peril facing the crew of the *Petr*?

(ii) Quote the lines that form the climax of this chapter.

(iii) What danger do you feel lies in store for the crew now? Give reasons for your answer.

(iv) How do you think they will meet this danger? Be prepared to give reasons for your answer.

2. **Appreciation**

Find words and phrases that convey:

(a) the danger, or

(b) the beauty of the scene.

3. **Discussion**

"The stolid calm and the intrepid nature of the Russian. . . which is so little understood by other peoples, was shown by the manner in which master and crew met the problem." (page 148) What is meant by this general statement about Russian character? Do you feel that generalized statements should be believed, or accepted, implicitly? Evaluate the accuracy of any other generalizations you may be familiar with.

4. **Related Activities**

(a) Art — Make a model of an ice pack.

(b) Research — In an encyclopaedia, read an account of the exploration of Vitus Jonassen Bering.

16 **THE LONG NIGHT** (pages 156 to 168)

1. **Questions**

(a) To what extent can you defend or sympathize with Kosiloff's attitude towards: (i) the eating of raw meat, (ii) the use of the otter pelts?

(b) If you had been Ivan, how would you have attempted to change Kosiloff's opinion in these two respects?

(c) Explain how Metek's diet provides a preventative (and cure) for scurvy.

(d) Apart from the danger of falling victim to the scurvy, what problems do the crew face? Illustrate your answer with references to the text.

2. **Discussion**

If you had been captain of the *Petr*, how would you have dealt with these problems?

3. **Related Activities**

(a) Creative Writing — In a short, written character study of Vatchel, indicate the function he fulfils in the development of the novel.

(b) Research — Most of the men who explored the North American continent had to contend with scurvy. Find out how the following explorers tried to prevent, and cure, outbreaks of this disease: (i) Jacques Cartier (Reference: *Dictionary of Canadian Biography*, Vol. I, page 168); (ii) Captain Thomas James (Reference: *Ordeal by Ice*, Farley Mowat, pages 119-127); Sir John Franklin (Reference: *Franklin of the Arctic*, by R.S. Lambert).

17. **MUTINY** (pages 169 to 178)

1. **Questions**

(a) Do you feel that the events of this chapter warrant its title "Mutiny"? (Look up the meaning of the word "mutiny" in the dictionary before answering this question, and illustrate your answer with references to the text.)

(b) Explain how the mutiny advances the plot of the novel.

(c) "They reminded him of a pack of huskies." (page 172)

(i) Discuss the effectiveness of Metek's description of the crew.

(ii) Had there been a good team spirit among the crew, in what different way might this chapter have developed?

2. **Discussion**

"Kosiloff's decision to eat raw meat is an example of man's instinct for self-preservation."

3. **Related Activity**

Creative Writing – Choosing *one* of the following purposes, write or be prepared to deliver orally, an account of what happened to the crew:

(a) a report for a North American newspaper,

(b) a notation in the *Petr's* log,

(c) a Russian radio announcement.

18. **DAWN** (pages 179 to 187)

1. **Questions**

(a) Do you feel that Kosiloff's change of heart is genuine? In answering, refer to the text.

(b) Discuss the reason for the weather being colder after the coming of the sun.

(c) Up to this point, what has been the greatest danger facing the crew? Give reasons for your opinion.

2. **Appreciation**

In pages 185 to 187, mention *three* devices the author has used to build up tension.

3. **Related Activity**

Art – Illustrate the "ice-monster" in a pop-art poster.

19. **RELEASED** (pages 188 to 197)

1. **Questions**

(a) Is Kosiloff's decision to keep Metek justified? Give reasons for your answer.

(b) Find evidence in the text to prove that Kosiloff's change of heart is permanent.

2. **Discussion**

(a) "Ivan is a realistic observer of a situation." From this and earlier chapters, give examples of his realism.

(b) "The element of chance which lands Metek at Eiber Village is too obviously a contrived happy ending to be convincing."

3. **Related Activity**

Show the film *Northern Dialogue*. NFB 0165057

20. **HOME AGAIN** (pages 198 to 203)
1. **Questions**
    (a) Why does the author bring Masumah back into the story?
    (b) What questions have been in your mind as you read and studied this novel?
    (c) What answers has the author provided to these questions?
    (d) Are any of your questions still unanswered? If so, hazard an answer yourself.

2. **Discussion**
    (a) "People are the same everywhere, at any time." Discuss, illustrating your opinions with references to the characters of *Iceblink*, and to people, fictional or real, of today.
    (b) "Conservation of Arctic game is unnecessary."

3. **Related Activities**
    (a) Research – Find out in what ways Eskimo life today is different from that portrayed in *Iceblink* in the 1750s.
    (b) Film – Show the film *Pangnirtung*. NFB 0159057